REDEEMING JUDAS

Finding Worth in an Age of Self-Doubt

STEVE JORDAN

Carpenter's Son Publishing

Redeeming Judas

©2018 by Steve Jordan

Published by Carpenter's Son Publishing, Franklin, Tennessee.

Published in association with Larry Carpenter of Christian Book Services, LLC. www.christianbookservices.com

Scripture taken from THE HOLY BIBLE, NEW INTERNATIONAL VERSION®, NIV® Copyright © 1973, 1978, 1984, 2011 by Biblica, Inc.™ Used by permission. All rights reserved worldwide.

Edited by Robert Irvin

Cover and Interior Layout Design by Suzanne Lawing

Printed in the United States of America

978-1-946889-97-3

For the hearts of my children.

"Above all else, guard your heart,
for everything you do flows from it."
—Proverbs 4:23, NIV

CONTENTS

Endnotes

PROLOGUE

The first thing that came to mind was the sweet smell of the grasses after the morning rain. With the sun young in the day, his mother would be outside, dusting off the pots she had left to dry overnight. He was toying with his sticks in the yard as he watched her. She was forever graceful in everything she did. There was a song in her sway, in her simple motion of dusting and slapping the pots with her rag. Even the dust seemed to swirl after she shushed it away. There was a peace there, in her presence. She may have been humming a psalm, or maybe it just seemed like it, but the song he remembered was serenity and warmth. He loved her. Her warm smile, her winks to him as he played with his siblings and chided them.

The knowledge he would one day work with his father caused regret. A large part of him wanted to stay, to be with her and the other kids inside, and watch her work. He wanted to hear her sing the songs of old, and watch her teach his sisters the ways of a good Jewish woman in an ever-changing world. A boy finds the soft place of safety in that environment. It is a place where the love of a mother fills the room, and where the lessons are largely for the girls. A boy escapes most of the learning of roles and religion at home—and he escapes the duties that call. To him it is theory, it is a fake world—and it has no pressure. The turn comes when he is caught hitting his sister for teasing him. The love that fills the room gets replaced by anger and scolding and tears.

Being the oldest was a challenge. The obligation of a first-born Jewish son was a bit too much for him at times. He honored his mother. Perhaps because of this, Judas was over-bearing and strict toward his siblings. Why cause mother any more strife? He loved the duty of being a mother's son, and he discharged that duty with diligence. The annoying habits of the younger brother and sisters, however, were beyond the scope of his patrol, and the picking and harassing would leave him no choice but to bite his lip and grit his teeth at their childishness. Patience did not come easy to the eldest, and he would snap at them for their misbehavior. But within just a few minutes of the scolding he would receive, all would be well again, he would forget his mistake, and harmony would return.

Amid the imagined turmoil of childhood, he had been given one gift from his mother that was alien to most of his caste: the ability to read and speak Greek. Beyond this, he was stabled in a corral of girlish youth. And he knew he must go to his father. There was another world to learn from, a world that he knew nothing of, but one that would shape him, mold him, and cast him into the man he would become. It was a world that would teach him other ways, even beyond what his father could.

A world he would eventually alter in a way no one could have fathomed.

THE OLIVE APPRENTICE

Judas watched his father manage something only a precious few had the skill to accomplish: acquire land. Under normal circumstances—if one could call the Roman occupation normal—the purchase of land was not a monumental task. It was a matter of forms, contracts, a voucher, and someone within the local ranks who would state a person's viability to the magistrate. In truth, the Romans could have cared more about the local goings-on in their conquered lands. But the soldiers and magistrates had seen so much conquest in their time that social happenings were scarcely a concern.

But in this province, under this particular magistrate, things proved much more difficult than they needed to be. The reason was the existence of God's people, in God's land, and a Caesar's watchful eye. This eye manifested itself in the local council and magistrate. In Jerusalem, and most of Israel, were pious men and women, but the concentration of these people in an outlying town like Bethlehem was always a concern for revolt, so the magistrate was thorough to the point of exasperation at the hint of any maneuvering—political or otherwise. The procurement of land was therefore scarce, save for inheritance, as disputes frequently sprang up regarding ownership, familial ties, even religious significance. The transfer of land in this case was a delicate matter. It was a larger tract—an overgrown and disregarded olive grove—and it was an estate sale. And considering the little money the Iscariots brought to the table, it would be no small miracle.

Originally from Kerioth, the Iscariots lived in a small community just north of Bethlehem. In the grand scheme of things, places like Bethlehem did not matter an iota to the Romans. Generally, the larger cities garnered their focus and control. Local governments were left to themselves to stumble through—so long as the taxes were paid and peace reigned. But first-century Jerusalem and the surrounding towns were under stricter observation. The Zealots were always attempting some sort of insurrection, and although it would theoretically begin in a city like Jerusalem, it was in the outlying areas where they solidified recruiting, trained, and orated their ways to overthrow the pagan Roman regime.

That the magistrates enjoyed exercising authority—condemning, curtailing, or seizing anything they wanted—indeed made this more of a miracle than a purchase. Rumors would swirl regarding the payments—or, rather, payoffs—which must have been included for a Jew with no direct ties to the ruling class or Pharisees to procure a farm.

However, truth is indeed stranger than fiction. Simon had known which statements to make, which buttons to push, and generally had a wisdom that transcended his fellow Jews. He would line up the facts as a lawyer would and state his case, and he would win. On the one hand, he was a proud Jew, with a thick family heritage documented well back into its storied history, but it was his command of the Roman customs that shone through when his turn to speak arrived. The Council seemed to turn up its collective noses toward him—until he began.

"I come here today," Simon said, "recognizing the greatness of Rome, of her fairness in allowing so much of my people's rituals to exist, and the incredible amount of latitude Rome has allowed, and in particular that your esteemed council has shown us. We Jews understand the need to maintain not only order, but also beauty for the province, and I stress a desire to tend to this blighted property as a necessity in preventing unwanted vagrants and wanderers from raping our land—and our tax base." There was no mention of the necessities of olive oils for his people or the money to be made. This was clearly a catering to Roman ego from start to finish, and it worked.

Less than wealthy and virtually uneducated, Simon Iscariot was still a man of respect. First-century Bethlehem was small, and news of men who aged well made the rounds. Simon had inherited his father's work ethic. As a tentmaker, potter, and sometimes farmer, Simon's father did whatever it took to feed his family of seven children; Simon was the youngest of three boys. He was one to impress his brothers and his father, opting to sneak from their home whenever possible to sit alongside his father in mending tents or forming pottery. He passed these stories to Judas, who loved them, devouring them in his mind as quickly as they were delivered.

Simon desired to be like his father, and he longed for the privilege of passing on stories of his life to his son Judas. This olive grove would be the way. Simon's ability to hide his paternal desires served him well. He focused not on what his son and he would gain together as much as what he could bring the community and his family name with a well-respected piece of land.

When he finished his pitch to care for this once-regal place that was quickly becoming blight, it seemed only fitting to the Council to grant his wish. It was magical; to Judas, it almost seemed as though the Council itself had dreamt the idea and called Simon in to appoint him as the property custodian.

The province conceded the property for a reasonable price, and Simon Iscariot became an olive farmer.

The grove was already in place and quite grown over when he made the purchase. Though work needed to be done, one could easily see there was a fantastic amount of care that had once been placed in the layout, the slope, and the logistics of the grove. The trees were sturdy and strong—the pride of an esteemed man. The previous owner was a man of respect, and if not for his speckled ancestry, many had said, the man would have been an elder of the Jews. There was no heir in his line, however, so the estate had fallen to the province, and it quickly sank into disrepair.

This was not too great a reach for Simon since farming was familiar to his line. Several generations of Iscariot men had farmed produce and herded various animals throughout the Mediterranean.

"The land is always willing to yield its fruit. It just takes the right man to harvest it," Simon would teach his son. "And this will be no different." Iscariot had the eagerness of a young man, though he was well into his forties, and his arms would reach deep into the soil. All of this left Judas proud to be an Iscariot. Though setting his home life aside was difficult, he accompanied his father to buying the tools needed. Grasping them for the first time, he felt a tinge of manhood and anticipation. Eagerness filled his young eyes.

In many respects, the people of the town saw the Iscariot men as a tandem to be heralded. One grown man bent on carrying on his family line as he himself had known as a boy, the other his oldest son—who carried the same demeanor as his father—with dark hair and skin tone just so. They laughed the same; their sense of humor was as identical as their eyes. They were quite a team, and they made quite an impression on the depressed community.

Judas found himself under the tutelage of a determined man in Simon. And the stress arrived for the son right away. There was a kind of tug of war at work—attempts to capture his father's attention and please him against the inexperience of youth. Simon knew he had only one chance at cultivating, massaging, pruning, and harvesting the family vision, driving this family name for the next generation. It would prove a monumental task. The silence around him seemed deafening for Simon at times; he knew he had an opportunity, for the first time, to do something significant. He could accomplish something on his own, just like his father and two of his brothers had. He would not take this chance lightly.

EARLY LESSONS

Like all young men, Judas needed to be baptized into hard work. The main problem in Simon's son was, essentially, a lackluster obedience. Too much time with mother and too little time in the fields with the men had done their collective damage. Judas found himself hurt frequently. The softness in his heart had been cultivated to a fine point, and the barking demands of Simon's instruction would pierce it quickly. His father's requests were strict, commands gauged by the work and timing needed to prepare for whatever harvest would be theirs. Judas's concern for himself was forcibly swallowed and beaten deep inside to produce the desired result of immediate obedience, submission, and focus. Farming was a cash crop business, and whatever men needed to do, they needed to do correctly, diligently, quickly. Placing the matter back in God's hands to bring fruit from their efforts must, by definition, be an efficient process.

Many a scolding came the young man's way. His father was

known as a jovial man, but once the business was theirs, Judas learned, through his father's focus, the seriousness of the task that lay ahead. Simon would begin rapid-fire dissertations on the olive business with his son, having gleaned so much from his own younger years of toil on various farms. In truth, however, though an owner of the land, Simon would be servant to the olive trees, slave to the harvest, subject to the weather, and beholden to still more: nature, insects, bugs, and the like. Over these battles Simon focused much of his time, attention, and teaching on his son.

Trenching needed to be learned, and done. No vineyard, farm, or grove is worth anything if it is not properly supplied with water, his father would instruct. Smaller trenches and furrows would need to be dug to supply each tree with enough water to sustain it, even in dry conditions. They could not be too deep or the water would pool and simply sink into the ground without continually flowing to its needed destination. Water would wander aimlessly unless channeled and disciplined to serve the grove, and Simon made sure Judas understood this as he checked every tree's domain from top to bottom. Rains and blowing storms with their wash of soil and gravel would change water routes and cut off vital circulation, and Judas needed to quickly recognize and fix this condition, his father taught him.

Another risk was root rot, which could result in loss of branches or entire trees themselves—a costly mistake if trees and roots were left unchecked or became damaged. There is no treatment for root rot, and it will ruin an entire tree within a season. Simon would instruct his son in the proper methodology to cover root systems, check the ground, mark areas where roots were visible, and take special care to never nick a root. Any open wound could cost them an entire tree, and the loss represented by that tree would never stop. There would be a hole in the row, and changes to soil structure would follow. It would take years to replace a tree, and Simon would have none of that.

There were many talks about tree care, not damaging trunks, caring for the bark, noting if damaged branches were worth sistering to other branches (tying to another branch for stabilization), or lopping off such a branch and carefully grafting it to another. One had to learn to evaluate a tree's ability to recover from a wound, a branch's chance of success after being damaged, and whether a tree could sustain the care of a wayward or damaged limb.

One had to learn to evaluate a tree's ability to recover from a wound, a branch's chance of success after being damaged, and whether a tree could sustain the care of a wayward or damaged limb.

The concept of grafting enthralled Judas. The idea of slicing into the ends of a damaged branch was no stretch. After all, if it didn't work, the branch would be tossed. But the idea of plunging an ax into a healthy trunk section just to save another one was risky and intricate—and yet Judas loved it. The aspect of control, a type of playing God, the nurturing and care—all of this brought him to life. Some men, his father explained, simply cut a V shape into the side of the trunk, stuck a branch in, and tied if off with cloth. The secret, Judas would learn, was to delve his knife into the ends of the branch in varying directions and to do the same inside the V cut, giving more space for the shoot to take.

This had to be done carefully, and wrapped extremely tight, with a tourniquet-like vise. Otherwise, too much air would make its way in, and too much moisture would gather—even with the cloth covering—and, once again, endanger the entire tree. Judas came to fall in love with the care of these trees.

Once the lectures were over—and to Judas, at times they seemed to stretch for days and days—attention finally turned to the trees themselves. Judas's appetite for work was finally being fed; even just talking of farming became enough to rouse the boy to action.

Once he began listening to his father, he adjusted quickly for a boy of ten. He learned to weed, to mound the dirt just so around the root systems and rows of trees, and spread gravel to prevent runoff when the rains came. The trunks themselves varied from medium to massive in size—of the latter, Judas could scarcely wrap his arms halfway around. Olive trees had notorious aboveground splitting trunk root systems. To Judas, these seemed at once beastly and beautiful.

Finally, he would learn which of the olives were ripe and ready, which needed to wait for its time, and which were rotten and needed to be thrown out. Naturally, he made many mistakes in this area, but eyesight, touch, and smell—all of these become his tools. After all, the fruit was the whole purpose of the grove, and Simon would have none of the tossing away of potential profit.

But pruning was Judas's favorite. It didn't happen much, but when it did, the boy jumped at the chance. He would wield his own ax and saw. Being trusted with instruments such as these signified a sense of arrival—he was no longer just a kid, he was a *partner*. He knew he could literally alter the shape of a tree with an ax and saw. He was

He knew he could literally alter the shape of a tree with an ax and saw. He was in charge.

in charge. He told the tree what it would do, which branches were worthy of keeping and which were sapping energy so vital for the rest of the tree that they had to go.

Judas was master of his domain, wielding blades that would cut his arm off if he were not careful.

A crisp draw of his saw once cut into Judas' finger so deep it nearly severed. Still ten—though in his mind a seasoned farmer—he could barely carry a sack full of olives. They would bump along his leg, which would bring a scolding from his father. All the same, the cut was a brutal reminder of his boy-hood. His father had taught him how to cut, of course, but Judas's blood spilling all over his clothes and the ground was a reminder that, as poetic as the union between father and son, the wisdom gap was yet to be fully bridged. It was a simple maneuver, the trimming of a branch, but like so many simple tasks, this one had a notch in just the wrong spot, causing just the wrong angle, and Judas found himself reaching over the branch with his right hand across his body. The saw caught, and in his haste and anger at his predicament he would yank just a bit too hard to free it. Simon was too far off, and he would be angry, Judas was sure, at having to halt his own work for such trivialness. Judas did not want help anyway; he wanted to prove his worth. He wanted to prove that he did not need to be rescued from a pinched saw, though the branch he was cutting into was as large as a man's leg. This pride would cost him a lot of blood.

The sound when the child is out of sight and in danger yet under one's care is never a good one. Judas's yell caused the normally placid grove and calm composure of Simon to immediately fray. Trees have a way of moving sound around, and Simon strained to remember which direction he had sent the young boy earlier that day. He ducked out of his tree and dropped quickly to the ground, as if the tree were on fire. He needed to find Judas's bag of supplies. Left on the ground at the base of a tree, it would indicate the boy's vicinity. Once spotted, he scrambled over to retrieve his son, who, fortunately, was only one lead branch up and still easily within reach.

Simon, trembling as he hurried him home, carried a mix of compassion and anger. How many times, he thought, had he told his son how to cut? Don't hold the branch in your hand close to the area you cut, and don't draw it toward your body. Don't press too hard against the tree. Let the saw do the work . . . Yet Simon also remembered that he could train his son only so much. The boy would have to learn from his mistakes if he was going to learn to listen well and, in so doing, learn to become a man.

> Simon, trembling as he hurried him home, carried a mix of compassion and anger. How many times, he thought, had he told his son how to cut?

It was a long trek home. Simon's legs were burning, and Judas began slipping in and out of consciousness. He would pass out several times that day—but doing so when his father carried him made dead weight of the boy, and the challenge to hold onto his son through sweaty hands and panicked steps grew exponentially. Simon was greeted outside the house after he yelled to his wife on approach. It was not a life-threatening injury, but the amount of blood loss and the screams that cut the silence added a level of adrenaline that Simon was unaccustomed to.

The needle they had to use needed washing, but the problem of blood itself was an issue. They couldn't see much in the cloth, and Simon himself wondered, in his haste to return home, if he hadn't accidentally torn the rest of the finger off. It was intact, barely, but enough to sew it back together. It would be crude, and a single finger might be basically insignificant. Judas had stopped screaming and was simply sobbing now, and as the adrenaline wore off, he promptly passed out again, only to be awakened by the pierce of the needle into his skin. His moments in unconsciousness, however, gave his mother and father the opportunity to secure him for the procedure.

He learned from this experience how to grit his teeth. This was a different grimace from any other scowl the boy had previously shown. The muscles in his young cheeks flexed their way, trying to find courage, but to no avail. The pain would be horrendous to a grown man, let alone a ten-year-old, and the scar would not heal well. But a valuable lesson was learned: Judas learned he could handle a lot more than he thought.

Ironically, after the incident Judas carried a renewed and larger sense of confidence. That is, once his hand healed and the bandage was removed. A confidence that he was now a man, having been baptized by his own blood, using a man's tool in a manner befitting men, and gaining for himself a reputation as a tough kid among his friends. Never mind that he passed out—that never seemed to make the story when he recounted his exploit to them. He just dealt with it, he would often say, just as any other man would. After all, it was just a finger; he had nine more! Such was his confidence. Even though there was a slight deformity Judas would carry the remainder of his life.

Judas had a reputation to protect, as every young boy does. He didn't cry when there was pain, just when father gave him a lashing. No, there was nothing, it seemed, he was not strong enough to do, and not too many other friends of his were faster. There were so many facets to conquer in becoming a young man, and Judas was mastering them all.

And when he wasn't too busy becoming a man, Judas humbled himself under his father's tutelage. After all, his father knew what had really transpired that day. How he had cried like a baby, held onto his mother for dear life, passed out, and then regained consciousness—only to whimper in her arms unceasingly until she was forced to leave her oldest son to attend to the evening meal. She would remark how funny it was that a single event could reveal a boy as still very much a boy—and yet mold him into a man at the same time.

3

THE HARVEST

The work to tender and harvest olives is both arduous and, at once, incredibly boring. Each tree has to be harvested by hand, cluster by cluster, either with a small hand rake or plucking one at a time. Occasionally, Simon observed his struggling son and would let out a clue: he would allow Judas to cut off smaller branches, which yielded the fruit, and beat them "as if they were The Great Adversary" in order to loosen the other olives to the ground. Even some rotten olives, he would instruct his son, could make good oil. They were often already on the ground, and each needed to be raked and gathered. Judas would learn, early, of the distinct differings between goat droppings and olives. But it could be difficult.

The younger trees they left alone, unless times were lean, but the larger ones received full attention. When harvesttime came during the fall, Judas and his father would arm the ass with layers of cloth left over from the estate, stained with husks and smudges of prior seasons, and several sacks for the olives;

they would then traipse off across the field. Once a starting point was reached, cloths would be spread out all around the base of the tree, until the edges were out of the range of the branches. In the fall, the olives turned from green to purple. It was quite a sight to see, and this changing of colors was God's way of making it obvious when a farmer needed to get to harvest.

But Judas spent his time as any boy would, and Simon would often have to help his son with the basics.

"Do not let the rake dig deep into the branches and pull more than necessary. Next year's harvest depends upon the preservation of the branch structure."

"Do not pinch the olives in the tines of the hand rake."

"Do not rake too hard and squash the olives."

He would argue—with little impact—to his young son that it was best to hand-pluck each olive and place it in his pouch.

Like any man, Simon knew his son would not stand for such painstaking work. There were dreams to be pondered, rocks to be thrown, olives to be eaten . . . It was bailing out water in a leaking boat, but Simon had little choice. None of his children, save Judas, were old enough even to walk to the grove without complaining, much less carry on the tasks needed to tend and harvest it. Besides, harvesttime would not wait for them, and he did not have sufficient community credit to hire extra hands.

Their first season there was some sympathy from the community. Though Iscariot pledged to care for the property, though it was in his blood, and though he paid for it, many from the community seemed to own the blight that beset them that first year. Men spilled forth from throughout the surrounding boroughs to help the cleanup, the harvest, and the pruning. It was as if their participation showed Simon just how important it was to them, and thus made the obligation to remain steadfast ingrained even deeper in his heart and mind.

But this was now their third season, and the community's desire to help had disappeared; Simon was sure, however, that their expectations had not. For some reason, one Judas would never know, the community had backed off the second year. Simon had many meetings and talks with the local men concerning the production from his property. There were those who wished to combine the oils the property produced with other products. There were merchants who stood to profit nicely from a local grove being harvested. Iscariot was a bit overwhelmed by it—and naturally backed off. There was a sense of paranoia in him, and this was manifested in the fear that someone, somewhere was going to be taking advantage of him. It fueled his suspicious nature and contributed greatly to his family's isolation by the end of the second harvest. The talks also seemed to frustrate him, and when he came back to the house after them, he never said a word. Never mind the risk of rotten oil—this was the cost of paranoia and not wanting to partner with people.

So it was man and son against time this third harvest, and the work remained incredibly tough. In truth, it was simple work, but when you are straining against seasons and underhanded, time always seems to find a way to win. Every olive yielded precious drops of oil, so each had to be handled with care. Judas had to fight the desire to just let the rake go over the cluster and the branches and watch the olives drop like hail onto the cloth, or to simply to beat the trees themselves indiscriminately. Inevitably, he would step on many a fallen olive, a cause of much frustration. He frequently would get the "this is not a winepress" lecture from his father, and with a sigh would resign himself to collecting the olives in his pouch. Every once in a while, usually around mid-morning and again in mid-afternoon, young Judas would slip a couple into his

> It was a small comfort when, inside his now thirteen-year-old analytical mind, his father had squandered potential help from the community with his greed.

mouth. The bitterness didn't bother him too much, and it was a needed shot of energy, a reminder for him that the true product was inside the olive and not the olive itself. It was a small comfort when, inside his now thirteen-year-old analytical mind, he realized his father had squandered potential help from the community with his greed.

Once the picking was complete, the trek back home and the unloading were all matters left to father and son. Judas grumbled to himself and actively wondered if his father had bitten off more than he could chew. After all, they couldn't possibly hope to do all of this work themselves. As the young man tired, his thoughts betrayed him all the more. As with most young men, only the first five minutes of a chore were fun. The rest was obligation, rote duty. The first season, there were many hands to help, and many a friendly conversation, but now at thirteen and lonely, the work was Judas's only constant companion.

There was a large tub that collected rainwater, and it served the function of washing the olives. Usually before they would return for dinner the washing would begin, then continue late into the evening. Judas was used to reading Scripture in the evening, or listening to the Psalms his father would recite. Harvest season set these exercises aside to deal with the task at hand. "A good Jew," his father would explain, "never misses on reading and reciting the Scripture." Yet there they were, forsaking piety for harvest season, year after year. "A small price. Even the Lord understands," his father would contend.

The estate's press was another matter altogether. After long days of picking, sorting, and washing, the press came next. Judas and his father alternated turning the press—working the millstones until they crushed the olives into paste, which tested the energy and patience of both Iscariot men to wait on the paste for its result. The oil drops needed to group to yield the most oil in the most efficient way. Judas barely had the strength required to turn the crank for long periods, and certainly wished he had older siblings to share this load. The desire to please his father receded beneath the sweat of labor, and the young man became his own champion through sheer intent and resolve.

> The desire to please his father receded beneath the sweat of labor, and the young man became his own champion through sheer intent and resolve.

The first season, the Iscariots all gathered as the millstones did their magic. One bushel was all it took, and they were processing. The excitement to see a finished product initially surpassed the wisdom of collecting and processing all at once. But like all eager investors, they needed to see fruit from their labor.

The early days were but a distant memory now, and the Iscariot men were left to their drudgery. The work would continue for several weeks. Once the pressing and separating was done, the millstones and disks that fit into the press needed washing. If not, the paste that they made from the olives would ferment in many areas, causing discoloration in the next batches, and thus quality problems. On some days, the Iscariot men would either stop picking altogether or send mother out with the other children to gain some ground in gathering—they knew this would be minimal, but at least something—while Judas and his father would stay home, clear and wash the millstones, and clean off or replace the hemp disks that were the mechanisms for the final product. Being an entrepreneur in the Israeli countryside was no light matter.

Judas quickly lost sight of his youth.

When it comes to a trade, the training of young boys into men can be likened to stuffing a mouthful of food into a baby's mouth while the infant is still chewing the previous bite. A lot spills out uneaten, untasted, and mostly wasted. There were many, many talks in those days. Walking to and fro, working and sweating together, the tired smiles and back-and-forth between the two would bond them in a way known only to them. Simon would pray and hope that the knowledge he was imparting about business, trade, and honesty was finding permanent nesting in the head of his eldest. There was much Judas didn't understand, but he was a keen observer. He could see the strain of the physical labor on his father's face. He could also see satisfaction.

He saw the strain of negotiating the sale of the products they had worked so diligently to produce. The difference in this strain was that it stole the satisfaction from a person. Judas did not like to see his father upset. He worked too hard. The men with whom he was negotiating obviously did not appreciate what went into producing the oil they were bartering over. In the end, there were equitable solutions, but the cost was always heavier than Simon wanted.

Budgeting took place for an entire season based on an agreed price for future product. The danger, of course, was economic trouble cascading on the people between price negotiation and harvesting. This happened every year, and if it was not an actual economic downturn everyone experienced, it was an imagined one, and the threat of price renegotiation was constant. It made forecasting nearly a futile effort. In the end, the price reached on the day of market in Simon's distribution network was significant; well over half of the year's production would come in at that price. The remaining portion was sold weekly to regular marketers and passersby. Simon and his son were fortunate to sell so much, so quickly, being one of the only producers locally, but they risked a bad price, and that was why the stress of negotiations was so high.

Judas's mother and sisters enjoyed selling some of their remaining oil, mostly in special casks they had weaved during the year. Both Judas and his father knew that what the women were doing was child's play by comparison. It brought additional money, but the largest portion either sold as soon as it was harvested or was marked at the harvest-date price. That price largely determined if the family would eat well and have new clothes for a year, or if new sandals and supplies would be it. "There is always next year," Simon would say.

Whenever they heard those words, the children knew the price hadn't been what was needed or desired, or both.

On more than one occasion those first few years, the temptation was to sell the now-fruitful, resurrected grove. When given a lower price for his oil than desired, this thought was further punctuated within Simon. The father knew it would save strife, but at the same time, beginning yet another career was a race against time he was not ready to stomach once again.

The experience, Simon told himself, was worth it for him—and more importantly for his son, his line, and his legacy.

THE JEWISH AIR

The struggles would continue for the family over the next few seasons. There had been a slight drought one year, and this unforeseen circumstance only added to a young man's misery. Not only did Judas have to help his father constantly, but also with less of a return; finding quality olives became an even more cumbersome job. The drought hit the olives hard, in particular because the fruit does not always produce an annual crop. Another year brought the olive fruit fly, which was a constant problem if olives were left on the ground. Another season saw a drop in the market price. Trees were also wont to get sick and develop galls, which corrupted the branches.

But the moths were the worst. That first season especially. Moths love to sit and breed and grow in the pruning. The grove was so overrun, and the previous owner (and opportunist passersby) had left many prunings behind. Perhaps this was the cause of the low price, Simon would often surmise. The Romans may have thought the place unable to salvage, and left Judas to pay just to clean it up, go bankrupt, and then they could repossess it from him and sell it again. The Iscariots would manage to make it through the moths, but they were true pests that persisted to cause some sort of difficulty every year.

Each of these challenges brought a need for prayer, but most times there were no answers, just a matter-of-fact mentality that left little choice but to wait out the circumstances. Judas's father wore his stress on his face as he began opening credit accounts where he could; these were in anticipation of the worst. Prayer was not prominently placed at the center of the family, unlike more devout Jews, and this was a curious item Judas thought about often, yet never shared. The doubts would shadow him. Was this a destiny carved out by his father as punishment from God? Was it that his father truly did not know what he was doing? Were they under a curse because of his father's attitude? Or was it just dumb luck?

Judas was also discovering he wasn't particularly religious in his own heart. God was real, he supposed, but to what degree and to what extent he was unsure. When push came to shove for Judas, as with many secular Jews, the whole thing was largely a story. If all anyone could do was tell stories, it wasn't worth getting worked up over. Some things just did not make too much sense when thought about practically, and Judas was growing up—and doing so in very practical ways.

He would often wonder how his friends were progressing in their training for the priesthood. Being thirteen and still doing the same things with no end in sight takes a toll on a young man. Anything seemed better than what he had to do—even if it meant following the dust of a rabbi and learning the Torah in intricate detail. At least, he told himself, the rabbis would not rant as his father did. In his current state, there would be no answers for Judas from a rabbi—his was to keep shuffling along at home.

In the grand scheme of things, as his father would attest, the biggest concern a Jewish man had was keeping the commandments, and raising his family to do the same. But Judas would quickly follow that statement with a qualifier: It was impossible to keep the commandments. So what was the use? If there was silence from God anyway, and a limited means of atonement . . . honestly, what was the use? The dilemma was accountability. No Jew really had accountability, what with God not striking anyone dead anymore, and distant priests offered nothing but guilt every time they came around. The yearly atonement rituals were attended only by the devout, and though many Jews did attend Pentecost, it was more a reminder, chore, or vacation than a sacred ritual to many of them.

Judas's father, unknown to the son, had planted the seed of cynicism in Judas's heart when he complained about the priesthood and the state of the Jewish nation. It was no wonder the boy grew up with little respect for clergy, which he rarely saw, considering the preconditioned state Simon had placed in him. But at the same time, Judas understood the priests' importance to his nation. Their presence was not only a reminder of God's law, it was a reminder of God's ability to show up at any time. They were truly a form of savior for the Jew, the pride of the Jewish people, and a reminder of God's presence—and His wrath. Regardless of his father's ravings, Simon was a blood Jewish believer, read the Torah, and would insist that his children read it—even if they never saw him touch the few scrolls in the family's possession. But there was always Judas's mother. She could always bring his heart back to softness with her singing. And the Psalms were there to remind Judas both of his humanity before God and God's heart to love him. All things considered, things could have been worse.

> Judas understood the priests' importance to his nation.

Many of Judas's friends had begun their formal studies in the Torah, and he was falling far behind. It was becoming more obvious that young Judas would never end up being chosen for anything other than farming. In truth, he wasn't sure he wanted to be trained in his family's faith anyway. It was an inheritance, after all, so what was the use in training in something unless the end result was a career for the people? Either way, most Jews had surrendered much of their living faith to the power that was really among them: making a living to survive in their Roman-controlled world.

A turn-of-the-century Jewish family in the Roman province that was Israel had to decide: be a thorn in the side of the Romans because they were trampling on hallowed ground that belonged to God, or sacrifice their faith for a lifestyle. There were the "true Jews" of the day, often called Zealots, who in as many ways as possible rejected the Roman occupation and made life difficult for the occupiers—but this often ended in their own violent demise. There were many others who resigned themselves to grumbling about their circumstances, but continued to live in them while making the most of their opportunities. On the one hand, men can strive to change their circumstances for the better—sometimes while being led by principle, others by selfish ambition. On the other hand, men can accept their circumstances as fact and attempt to flourish under them regardless. This was the majority decision for the Jews of Israel in the first century. It was also the decision of the Iscariot men. But to Judas, it was almost a ruse: claiming a faith, even claiming a God, when in reality almost all the Jews he had ever met lived as if God were a concoction of man's imagination. Circumstances had the upper hand, and since God had been silent for hundreds of years anyway, circumstances would win.

> The debates were heated: did God allow these circumstances because of Israel's sin? Where was the Messiah, who was to come into the picture and bring glory back to Israel?

The debates were heated: did God allow these circumstances because of Israel's sin? Where was the Messiah, who was to come into the picture and bring glory back to Israel? Were the Israelites in sin to comingle with their pagan occupiers? In all, the environment was ripe for talk, ripe for loud men with loud voices, even those whose hearts were not as stout as their words. True faith was something talked about heavily. The smug among them often spoke of God's justice and the eventual victory of Israel, of her virtues and the need for patience. Most of the older men spoke this way—that is, when they spoke. These were the men who looked into the eyes of the mothers, the security of the children. They believed in the necessity of the Jews not being annihilated because of some foolish Zealot-led crusade that the Almighty had not endorsed.

Whether patient, wise, or eager, everyone sought a leader who would engage the men to act. Whether that action was for unity for peace under the circumstances, or unity to carve out a Jewish state that would force the Romans' attention and acquiescence—nearly everyone had a desire for God to move in some way. It was not enough for the Jews to have peace in their time and pay taxes (many would say homage) to their Roman captors. To many, the circumstances were a call to arms. There just wasn't a galvanizing force to make it all happen.

These voices, these discussions of action and passion, were not wasted on the young Judas. Compared with the painful drudgery of olive picking and the constant bickering and jockeying for mother's attention by his siblings, talk of secret rebellion and secret societies of men made his heart rapt with desire. Judas was changing. Simon could see it. He knew, as his son grew, he would have a fire inside him that could not be quenched,

> But a father's real fears lie in the twinkling of a son's eye that says, "I want to be important."

a desire to do something—anything—to make life better for his family, for the people. But a father's real fears lie in the twinkling of a son's eye that says, "I want to be important." To a Jew, this pride was a tough fit under the canopy of service to God—whether as a rabbi's pupil or a businessman or a farmer. Pride was a surefire way to quench the blessings of God, and it was pride that Simon saw growing in his son's eyes.

Simon had plenty of time with his son, and plenty to give him in this regard. "Diligence is the maker of a man," he would tell Judas. "Olives don't pick themselves because a strong man shakes the foundations of the earth or rattles the tree loose of its fruit by a thunderous voice. The wise man seeks the slow, deliberate path using the gifts God has given him—his hands." The pressing millstones pasted the olives, and the patience of wisdom watched as the oils collected themselves into groups of drops for extraction. "All this is a gift of God," Simon would teach his favorite son. "And no gift can be enjoyed in haste." Whatever the market gave them was from God, and what was withheld, likewise. Judas, when he listened, would note the wisdom that came from work. He knew that, though his father wasn't well educated, he certainly knew much about life.

Still, the talk of faith "lived" and executed in the form of extreme passivity stirred Judas's anger and discontentment like nothing else. The problem for Judas, as with most young men, was that the wisdom of aged men was counterbalanced by the necessity of personal significance. Judas heard every word of his father's regarding work, and he kept it close to his heart. But the drive for significance was deep within him, and it would not rest.

> Still, the talk of faith "lived" and executed in the form of extreme passivity stirred Judas's anger and discontentment like nothing else.

The economic struggles would continue. As the days wore into months that third year, and the frustration of a struggling family business grew the light of optimism dim in his mother's eyes, Judas began to see futility in the "wisdom" that had carried his family down this path. Fear was beginning to creep in. He did not want to become a rabbi; it was a long shot for him anyway. And he certainly didn't want to own a failing business.

He had lost the heart of a learner of principle, and had

begun to trade it for the heart of adventure.

To a Jew in Judas's day, there were three levels of honor. One, of course, was to honor God. A good Jew did this by keeping the commands to the best of his or her ability. "There are more than six hundred commands to be concerned with," Simon would teach Judas. The weight of the matter kept him in line, but the impossibility of keeping them also let him off the hook. The second level of honor for a Jew was to honor the group with which a man's family had identified. People almost always end up affiliated with a group. Judas and his family had spent considerable time with the Sadducees; with their lax attitude toward purification, it made sense for a working-class family to align with this group. In terms of their actual status, however, it would have made more sense to align with a lower group, such as the Pharisees, but this was not to be.

Finally, the honor that, in reality, submitted to the other two was that of honoring family. It was ironic, given what the Torah spoke of about honoring father and mother, but the family unit itself ranked third. The Jews may have publicly belonged to a certain group, but woe to the man who did not honor his family. When push came to shove, family won. There was always enough in the form of ties to family to bind a man by his word.

The true experiment for Jewish honor, however, came when the integration of the race met up against the hormonal challenges of a young man. Judas honored his family with his love and his labor, but he was also anxious.

ON KEEPING SCORE

"Don't judge a man by his opinions,
but what his opinions have made of him."
—Georg Christoph Lichtenberg[1]

Our minds hold amazing amounts of information. I recently told my ten-year-old that research today theorizes the memory capacity of the human brain is approximately 2.5 petabytes, or 2,500 terabytes. That's the equivalent of the data needed to create . . . 2.2 trillion puppy pictures. To this, my daughter responded, incredulously, "So we're smarter than computers?!" Well, maybe not so much. Quite a bit of the material stored in our brains is useless, mundane, and some of it is in constant use, whether we know it or not. The other material is conjured up only at specific times.

Our brains are amazing devices, and they store information not only through the senses, but interpretations of the sensory information we receive, thoughts that follow or layer upon thoughts, and thoughts that follow feelings. There are endless *if-then* scenarios that we play out in our minds about any given subject, only to shake our heads and seemingly erase those mental wanderings as we snap back into reality. If one stops to think about it—no pun intended—there is so much junk floating around in our brains that it's dizzying— and practically infinite.

Despite all that, there are core beliefs that fix themselves as mainstays in our lives. There are core responses—some would call them knee-jerk reactions—that accompany these beliefs. It is important to note that these responses may or may not be rational. We may dismiss these reactions and responses when they pop into our heads; we may even think we are controlling them. But they are there, and they can actually grab our life rudder whether we're conscious of it or not. They can guide us into areas we normally wouldn't go, into situations we normally wouldn't find ourselves, and into associations we normally wouldn't entertain.

> We can view ourselves through lenses and core beliefs that may or may not be true.

Beyond all the brain-stuff data out there, we can safely say that we view ourselves through lenses and core beliefs that may or may not be true. The danger is that we are not sure whether we are listening to truth, but we obey the self-talk anyway. How many times, given a situation, do we say, or think, "That's not for me"? Or, "I can't do that"? Or, "That will never be me"? We see someone else try something new and we remain stuck in our own personal ruts, dismissing our possibly stepping out on faith as . . . an impossibility.

Putt-Putt

I want to suggest a paradigm. Think of the relatively simple game of Putt-Putt golf. At the game's outset, everyone gets a club, a colored ball, and a scorecard. On the scorecard, you have a box for "par" on each particular hole. Everyone, regardless of who they are, gets the exact same scorecard with the exact same par values. In other words, under normal circumstances, the standard score to get past the windmill, around or between the blue water, and in the hole is, say, three strokes. If you do it successfully, you "make par." If not, well . . . let's just say there is no lower version of golf than Putt-Putt. So maybe cards are your thing. What I'm seeking to draw attention to is that the assessment tools for success—the scorecard and the accompanying par values—are the same for every player.

While many works have become popular regarding self-talk, self-image, and self-reflection, what is missing for many of us is a healthy, non-judgmental assessment of where we are coming from, where we currently are, and where we're going—our own par value. In other words, maybe our personal scorecards don't reflect our starting points: our hurdles, obstacles, or delays between us and our objective. In life, schools, teachers, aptitude tests, and even our family members preload our scorecards with par values for life. Life success is often defined, quantified, and set as expectations by others, and then adopted by us—and most of the time with no questions asked. I am middle-aged, seemingly healthy, from a middle-class family. I possess a measure of intelligence (my sisters might say questionable!) and therefore, in a fairly free culture and country, I should be able to achieve X, Y, and Z without too much trouble if I just do A, B, and C! But the typical scorecard needs to reflect more than just the basic information found in a survey or standardized test. Are both parents present? Is there abuse in the family? Is there addiction in the family? Additional childhood trauma? What is the surrounding community like? These factors present hurdles in life—hurdles in processing certain information in certain ways. They add strokes to the given par three, in other words, and turn the hole into a bigger obstacle. Maybe it should take five putts to get the ball into the little hole.

It's a funny thing talking with my kids these days. When something is done that sets a sibling off, one of the kids—usually the one that rhymes with "my son"—runs around the house saying, "Triggered!" But where did the kids get that term? Media, movies, and friends of course. But where did it come from to make it into those forms of our culture? It comes from counseling circles, where there are things that happen that "trigger" deeper emotions and memories. In attending training classes for adoption and fostering, I've learned that it is amazing what can trigger a child (who is normally placid) into a rage or send them cowering into a corner. Experts have learned through research that smell is the strongest of the senses when evoking memories of trauma. I can tell you that, growing up around a lot of alcohol, smelling beer on the breath of another person still brings back memories for me, and these trigger some changes in my mood, heart rate, and actions. To others, it's just a need for a breath mint! Different par value on the scorecard.

There are no simple solutions to dealing with core beliefs, memories, and responses. I think this much is clear: there are fewer and fewer people in today's society who can truthfully say they have no pre-wiring in their minds, no past happenings that skew, in one way or another, what goes on in their minds. The people I will feature in this book, who I have interviewed in detail, are champions of dealing with these core issues and still functioning well in our fast-paced society. As anyone who has chosen the hard path of mental recovery can attest, retracing mental steps to their core, initial actions and circumstances, and recalculating a personal scorecard while still twirling the plates of life—well, it's a daunting task for anyone, one not to be taken lightly.

So are we just to throw in the towel on doing anything new based on our normal scorecards? Because, if we search for something wrong in our lives, we can find excuses for lots of things that come our way. No, to throw in the towel would be childish. What we *can* do is change our scorecards to reflect the starting point on a given hole, and proceed with the end in mind, now holding a sober assessment that we are not PGA professional material! Maybe we shouldn't flog ourselves if it takes us four strokes on a three-stroke hole. This is commonly called giving ourselves grace. It is unnatural for many of us to be anything other than critical of ourselves, constantly correcting our courses of action until we bend to a mold of whatever par value has been given by culture or at least those around us. I think this is what's important: par for the course is actually to *complete* the course, not to measure up to a predetermined number or path. So we aren't off the hook, but we shouldn't demonize ourselves along the way either.

> Par for the course is actually to *complete* the course, not to measure up to a predetermined number or path.

It may be par for the course for a "typical kid" to make it through college. Yet for some, who have had significant hurdles, it takes much more to just enroll. There's a great scene in the movie *Tommy Boy*. I'll never forget the scene when Tommy, the bumbling and accident-prone character played by the late Chris Farley, makes it back from college. David Spade, the accountant and Farley's childhood friend, remarks sarcastically that Tommy graduated with his bachelor's in "just a shade under a decade." Farley remarks that plenty of people go to school that long. Spade replies: "Yeah, they're called doctors." Different expectations and par values. Tommy was challenged a bit mentally, at least according to the so-called norm.

I should tell you a bit more about myself. People looked at me, going to college, living my life, and saw a typical kid doing what millions of others do. On the surface, they were right. But I was going to college on a scholarship provided me by the death of my father when I was seven years old, and I was in the throes of one of the most destructive times in my life with drugs and alcohol. Growing up in an alcoholic environment after my father had passed, my view of myself, my surroundings, and therefore my scorecard was far different than many others. I had disadvantages, voices of discouragement embedded in my mind, and yes, personal dreams—but no fuel or encouragement. It took years of mistakes, talking, counseling, and the undeniable patience of my wife and those around me to be able to change my scorecard. Perhaps if I had a different path through my youth, my scorecard and personal expectations would have been different. As it was, for me, just making it to class in college was sometimes its own victory. So . . . a change in the scorecard. Comparing myself to all those around me who seemed happy and well-adjusted would have made me that much more miserable. I still had to take respon-

> Comparing myself to all those around me who seemed happy and well-adjusted would have made me that much more miserable.

sibility and do the work, but the starting points were different. And school took me a bit longer. By the grace of God—and some jail time—I made it, while adjusting my scorecard along the way until I was comfortable with my par.

As we journey through Judas's story and watch him follow his path, we're going to be introduced to a few people—people who had staggering hurdles placed in their paths. They had incredible handicaps—and thus scorecards—to work with. When I realize what each of these people had to face in order to continue their life travels, it gives me a greater appreciation for the journey all of us are on. Perhaps you'll begin assessing yourself differently: from keeping score through other people's expectations and being unfair to yourself, to a shift of understanding that sometimes the little victories in life are worth celebrating. That gradually building your momentum to being able to tackle the windmill and blue water trap perhaps should be handled differently than others. All of this also might give us a greater understanding of those in front of us who are going a bit slower than our liking.

Being comfortable in our own skin is important, and for some that is the journey of a lifetime. Truly working toward change only comes when we know where we are working *from* and where we are working *to*. If we use Warren Buffett's scorecard for investing, or Steve Jobs's scorecard for running a company—well, let's be honest: we'll be setting ourselves up for much disappointment. Stories from others can be warnings, inspirations, and examples, but when it comes to walking our days on earth, we have to make sure our scorecard is *ours*. We have to be able to judge our actions accordingly, improve where we can, and assess things fairly and accurately, through the lens of our experiences and through the lens of a living, loving God. And if we aren't solid in faith, we can lean on others, who can provide pillars for us as we journey. Most of all, what we need is a fair and accurate scorecard.

I used to think I would be retired by the age of thirty. My reasoning? I saw *Wall Street* with Michael Douglas. I would easily be able to use the stock market to make it. I loved nice things, and I loved money. I had a subscription to the *Wall Street Journal* in high school. What more could it take? Then reality set in. I was growing up in the mountains of Wyoming, and I had zero connections and zero working capital. I also lacked the necessary kill-or-be-killed attitude. Other than all of that, I was set: I was equipped with my dreams but had no reality, no money, and no real plan. I needed a different par on my scorecard. Perhaps I needed a bit more knowledge. But really, I needed to be far more grounded in who I was, what I wanted, and what I was all about.

After being married and having kids, I didn't find myself fully surrendered about my new life as a father and husband until our third child! I was still holding onto an old scorecard, one in which I could have my career, wife, kids, faith, be rich, and everything would just be hunky-dory. It wasn't until I realized that, no matter what else happened, I was always going to be a husband and a father, until the day I died, that I finally recalibrated things and changed my scorecard—and thus my value system. It is a level of surrender I am now happy to embrace.

Rather than chasing after significance, career, or other pursuits, I am engaged with my wife and kids, and much less frustrated. This has also made me a more effective husband and father. At least, that's what I think.

Having spent time with youth in ministry work, I was able to see a broad spectrum of behavior and family life of the many teens in our ministry. I will never forget sitting down to consistent, normal family dinners as a guest—and not being able to understand what was happening around me. It was like a TV show. Only it was real; it wasn't put on as an act for the sake of me, the guest. Other times I visited with families living in two-bedroom apartments. These families had no father and three to four siblings and were barely making it. Different pars, different starting points. I have been able to see people from all walks of life, from rich and spoiled to homeless, walk the same path of faith. I've watched people wisely adjust their scorecards and ultimately finish their various tasks along the way, and I've seen others fail. I have developed deep respect for those who struggle and overcome, and deep respect for those who struggle and try again.

> I have deep respect for those who struggle and overcome, and deep respect for those who struggle and try again.

It is incredibly humbling to hear myself complain after I meet people who faced far higher hurdles than I did. About fifteen years ago, my wife and I drove an Indian missionary and his wife across Ohio to attend a conference. As we drove north, I hit a pothole on Interstate 71. My knee-jerk reaction was to complain about the ridiculous condition of the roads. I complained. To the missionary. From India. He had roads paved with mud and dirt, roads complete with bicycles, elephants, massive smog, dirt, people walking, others on mopeds, motorcycles, and some cars, and still others riding rickshaws. All on the same road. No dashed lines. People everywhere in every direction. And I was complaining because I hit a pothole. Different scorecard altogether.

We need to be watchful for ourselves and our sanity as we walk through life. When we are hit with tragedy, or gripped by fear, anger, shame, guilt, or depression—when our scorecard should adjust with a more gracious scale—we live on a far higher plane if we acknowledge these things and move forward accordingly.

THE ROMAN PROBLEM

Nearly all Jews faced an important issue: a lack of understanding of their own customs and laws. Being illiterate meant little when it came to growing crops or, really, anything having to do with general labor. Where it mattered most was in understanding the intricacies—or perceived intricacies—of a people's own customs. Knowledge was a king of sorts for the Hebrews, particularly because control of the Jewish populace and mind-set was of the highest importance to maintaining their peace under Roman rule. A certain threat from the populace would come when someone would read their laws, grasp the Messianic prophecies, and attempt to build for themselves a force that might mimic the coming Messiah.

One such man in Judas's lifetime was Octavian.

Octavian was obnoxious. He was a half-breed, to be sure. He was a scourge of the pure race. He had a Greek mother and a father who was a Jew. Half-breed Jews came in two classes. One would have a whore for a mother: an adulteress who married a pagan, which many Jews saw as grounds for stoning. The second class would have a father as a Jew and a pagan mother. This meant being ostracized—the father had no honor left. It was another symptom of a people fallen from grace—labels and societal tiers for the corrupted among them. Octavian at least had a Jewish father. That reality allowed him the precarious license to speak, and often be heard, by the young men known as the Dead Sea Sect.

In these days, there were many groups to contend with in Jerusalem and her surrounding areas. The Pharisees were middle and lower class priests who held significant sway among the Jewish populace, though their numbers were few. The Sadducees held the main control of the temple and sacrificial rites, but outside that they paid no mind to the righteousness—or lack of it—among the people around them. The Essenes were even further removed, though they were perhaps the most ceremonially clean of all the religious groups. They managed to clean themselves many times per day, and no one really understood why. Most would joke that they were trying to clean off the Jew, since the Jews could not help but fall under the wrath of God or a raiding party—whichever came first.

There were, of course, scores of other groups, just as there were opinions and families and homes. Jerusalem was thick with itself, with its neighbors, its customs galore, and its multitude of regulations. One scarcely could walk the streets without breaking some ordinance of some group here or there. The result, naturally, was that no one ended up caring a great deal. It was just more distraction to deal with.

The Dead Sea Sect, however, snared many a fancy, particularly with the young people. There was a hint of faith and courage to their words, and the elder men of Jerusalem who had not completely died inside would bend an ear to their speeches. But it was the youth who were most attracted to this group. They had not yet been educated in the fine art of getting along in a hodgepodge of a culture like Jerusalem, and they would care little about stepping on toes. Making the venture to a camp of the Dead Sea Sect, however, was an entirely different matter. It was safer to agree with their rhetoric than join them. But it was still a delightful escape to hear the preachers of this sect.

Octavian's speeches might go something like this:

"Youth is vigor, and vital to Israel's survival. Without the untainted vigor, faith, and conviction of Israel's youth, we are destined to be subjects of pagan nations for eternity. Now is the time for young men to capture their moment, to seize their time and the opportunity to do what no man has yet to do—imitate the Great King David and unite the people to crush our enemies under foot."

But once a Roman centurion made his way around the corner, the radicals—including the rabid Octavian himself—vanished from sight. So much for the power of speech. Maybe these people wouldn't literally flee, but anyone could see their cowardice revealed like a cockroach caught in the candlelight. The centurions found ways to reveal everything. Some "bravery," some "faithful vigor"—these men all cowered at the sight of the Romans. Judas didn't seem to have much trouble seeing through the young zealots whenever the family ventured to Jerusalem. Judas seemed to have a keen interest in watching people.

But sweating in the heat with his father, actually farming the trees, and seeing, firsthand, what a good fruit was—all of this rubbed off on Judas as well. His father had done his part. Manual labor had given Judas some degree of wisdom, and he steered clear of the boys and young men who seemed concerned about themselves and their place in their people's history. They were just talkers and deceivers, and they were bent on self-indulgence for grandeur. Judas did not bother avoiding them. Their obnoxious chanting about everything was just another reminder, Judas often thought, of the silence of God.

Being a great people with an even greater history—broken and battered though it was—was also a great curse. Any semblance of organization that was an offshoot of the faith was seen as a blessing from God, but it also needed to be conscripted with priestly acceptance. The Jews had worked hard to protect and defend what little they had, and the ridicule and slaps to the face stacked up for them a tradition, rich with its rules, that most certainly needed to be adhered to. It was all they had to hang on to, given the fact that an official state was something they no longer possessed. Any man who would dare question the elders of a town on matters of God and law, ritual and tradition, met with a stern rebuke.

Even if the rebels and revolutionaries (as they were often secretly called) made it past the gauntlet of priestly knowledge and rule, there was certain humiliation awaiting the imposter at the hands of the Romans. The Roman soldiers kept a watchful eye on the Jews, especially the younger ones. For the Romans, their kingdom was based largely on keeping peace with the peoples they had conquered. And the Roman soldiers were too stout for a small band of feeble Jews to deal with effectively anyway. The Romans were inclined to allow local rule to continue, local customs to stay, and local code and laws to remain intact—save for the payment of taxes to

Caesar, which must be added to them. It was simple, really: take over the lesser peoples and build an empire of management. They also knew, however, it was important to keep certain peoples under control.

Legendary stories abounded, even in Rome herself, of the Great Jewish God. This God, many would say, was not to be trifled with. The stories of old—of splitting seas and dividing rivers and conquering the mighty Egyptians, among others—made their way into the halls of Rome and her senate. While seemingly a long way off compared with the majesty that was Rome, the stories still lent an air of caution when considering the best course of action with the Jewish colonies. In truth, the Roman government had little care or concern for Jews. But military opinions often were keyed on the insecurities of the rulers, so decisions were made to ensure a constant presence and fast military response in the event of any uprising. It was not as if there was any Jewish *faith* among the Roman rulers; it was a matter of efficient governance and profiteering in peace.

Meanwhile, the Jewish elders, with all their posturing, were busy fighting among themselves as to how to divvy up the care of the faithful. The liberal ones among them, usually the younger, thought it best to surrender themselves to the structure the Romans had set up—so local authority could mirror the jurisdiction of the Roman sentries and magistrates. This would enable the Jews to speak the language of the pagans when needs or problems arose. (After all, one could not expect the Romans to understand or appreciate the Jewish laws.) It was a matter of a peace offering, per se, and a way to remind the Romans they were peaceful subjects.

The argument made a certain amount of sense to the older men, but it was a hard sell. After all, though the elders believed, to a man, that God was cursing the Jews (it wasn't without precedent), God did not want mixing going on—at least, not much. They were far more comfortable—and more in control—if the leadership ranks, style, and substance came from their own rulebook. God had shown great disdain when, centuries before, Israel asked for a king. The elders knew the people were growing more into citizens with the world than remaining a peculiar people belonging to God. They knew that if they had even a shred of dignity, they would at least try to keep the commandments and traditions.

> The elders knew the people were growing more into citizens with the world than remaining a peculiar people belonging to God.

In fact, their traditions and laws were the only authority the priests could use on the people. And use and flex them they did. If the people began to drift openly toward the current political situation, if they began to adhere to local structures, they would lose what little leverage they had. So the Jewish leaders did what wise leaders do: They had meetings in secret with the local magistrate and built a friendship that might be likened to a rope bridge between cliffs.

There was something about the hearts of men meeting in secret that was particularly tantalizing to a Jewish priest. They were expert negotiators—after all, so many encounters that might have ended in their slaughter left them faring better than other peoples because of them. The Hebrews were physically small people, and the stories of their exploits and military victories certainly didn't match their stature. The need to negotiate was always before them. Their own history was an art form, one worth learning from. They would paint themselves as a sort of police group so as to "not be a bother" to the Romans. Their occupiers could assign less troops that way. And what a coincidence that would create. Although, on the one hand, the priesthood and council would not want intermingling, they now found their authority not from God but from the Romans. Their tentative relationship would see its test over the next generation—and that bridge would eventually burn. But that wasn't known at this time; the Jewish leaders forged ahead.

There was a dual purpose in the negotiations: the benefit of the overall Roman state and the side deals contrived in secret for payment of taxes and other levies. It was advantageous for a Roman magistrate to have a city of peace and to understand, at least on a cursory level, the Jewish customs. After all, having a Jewish priest address and explain the Roman ways and taxes to the brethren, and even collecting those taxes, made life easier on the magistrate. He would lose his job, his citizenship, or his life if he failed, and yet he might live on—and even become wealthy—if he played his role in a certain fashion.

These interwoven facts and motives laid a foundation for the Jews, their people, and their ultimate destruction at the hands of the Romans.

A Friend

There was always a long period of downtime after harvest. The trees were alone again, left to recover, lick their wounds, and regroup themselves in their tireless way. But downtime just meant more work at home. The millstones needed cleaned and the fiber replaced or repaired on the disks. Though care was taken throughout the season, once harvest was complete, there was a more thorough examination and cleaning that took place. That short straw belonged to Judas. He would painstakingly scour and scrub the stones to ensure no oil or olive parts remained. It was vital, not just for the life of the stones, but for the stench that rotten olives left. Additionally, there was the painful lesson of the insects that would be attracted to the shed if care was not taken.

After the stones, the disks that did the collection of the oil were next. Sometimes Simon and Judas would decide to discard them—they were made of hemp or other fibers, and inevitably they would wear. The lesson here was constant care.

Judas became an expert in keeping these disks clean. The cost added up for everything left to chance, and this was one area through which a little extra effort could put money back in the Iscariot coffer. In drought times or lean economic times, little things meant a great deal.

With these items done and the harvest truly over, Judas was allowed to spend time in "town," as he called Jerusalem. There weren't many noteworthy boys around the grove or Bethlehem, but Judas had freedom to venture into the city, and venture he did. Simon had one surviving sister, and she was a widow. Her pride and joy was her only son, Pesach, born just three days before Judas. He lived in northern Jerusalem, a short jaunt for a young man from Bethlehem, and it was here that Judas escaped as often as possible. They weren't close as friends, but they were family, and the connection was enough to give Judas his launch into the lively Jerusalem scene.

Trouble for young Jewish boys was not trouble as understood by their pagan neighbors. The latter would steal, cheat, and tease total strangers. Jewish youth, on the other hand, would stick to the normal vices—being late to everything, wandering all over creation, and generally fooling around too much for their own well-being. They would distract and tease shop owners, old ladies, and the like. Gambling was not out of bounds for them, either. And every once in a while, they would sneak the occasional apple from the marketplace cart, but even Jewish boys generally had a conscience to the monitoring that was done by the Romans. Jews carried a healthy sense of guilt anyway.

> Jews carried a healthy sense of guilt anyway.

Jewish boys within a given province were taught by the local rabbis, who had handpicked their disciples through a series of lectures, tests, the study of personalities, and histories of families of boys in their area. They taught the boys not only Torah and Mishnah, but also customs and traditions needed for godly boys to grow into reverent men.

For most of the boys, it was mere teaching upon teaching.

Their fathers were concerned with status, and highly competitive. So desirous were they to see their sons placed with the best rabbis that many of them believed heavily in training themselves—and also heartily believed in donations to their favorite rabbi. The behavior was a mixture of piety and covetousness. It was not so much out of respect for God as it was about pecking order, status, and to avoid being viewed or perceived as a community embarrassment. What good Jew didn't teach his son? And what Jew wanted to answer in the negative if asked a penetrating question?

Simon Iscariot wasn't too concerned with impressing anyone, nor for his son to be taught by a top rabbi, or any rabbi, for that matter. Torah was part of their times together, but more often the duties of the grove took precedence, particularly during harvesttime. Simon was no longer a young man, and the grove took its toll on him—so much so that, at times, Judas found himself ahead of his father in the morning.

> Torah was part of their times together, but more often the duties of the grove took precedence, particularly during harvesttime.

Though praying the prayers required was occasional, when it struck his father's fancy, the truth of the faith would run deep in Simon's heart. Judas would be pruning, or picking, or attending to any number of tasks, and he would listen to the recitation of the psalms from his father's lips while he worked, and even more frequently, to a song in praise to his distant God. What Simon did not practice and instill directly into his son, he did manage to remind him through song.

The lack of spiritual drive from home was not a large matter in Judas's relationship with Pesach. The Jews generally stuck together, and the culture of business and religion was deep within the Iscariot clan. Pesach had been chosen by a respected rabbi and had been in tutelage for more than a year. There was an irony here. Pesach loved to hear the stories of the grove and longed for the peace of the countryside. Judas attempted to sway his mind otherwise, noting the hard work and diligence needed in the field. But Judas's words only proved to romanticize the affair for his cousin as they wandered through the seemingly endless boroughs of Jerusalem.

Though it was not a focal point of any visit, Judas did manage to procure some spiritual relationships, something he was actually quite good at. He learned all the customs when he would visit town, and he had befriended several of the clergy—a side benefit of having a cousin in tutelage and spending time in synagogue praying for the grove. One clergyman he found a commonality with was Hillel, himself a student of the great Gamaliel. Hillel had been named after Hillel the Elder, who was, in many respects, the Jews' modern version of Moses. The name was common among those who followed him.

Hillel and Judas had met innocently enough. It was a brief stop in the marketplace that saw Gamaliel engaging in a spirited discussion; Jewish theology was ever spirited. Hillel took a seat, and in customary seventeen-year-old fashion, half paid attention to his rabboni discourse about laws that he knew front and back.

It is at this very point that Judas and Pesach happened upon the scene. Their interest made Hillel smirk.

He leaned toward Judas: "Same as yesterday. You're not missing much." Pesach wandered a bit to the side, leaving Judas alone with a new friend.

Judas smiled with a slight touch of insecurity. "Ha. We must have missed that one." Playing cool was new to Judas, but he caught on quickly. It startled him, and up to that point, Judas realized he and his cousin had been wandering around without speaking a word to anyone all day. He was quite unprepared for this conversation. Hillel was just the opposite.

He asked if Judas knew the verses Gamaliel referred to. Judas did. So once Judas explained the Scriptures, he opened up a bit and relaxed. He now leaned nonchalantly on the closest fruit stand. Judas may not have been from the city, but he did have confidence. The two exchanged names, and Hillel asked where he was from.

"Is it that obvious?" Judas quipped.

Hillel was almost apologetic in his reply. "Oh no, it's not that. It's just that . . . I don't know. I could just tell you weren't from around here."

Judas explained his circumstances to Hillel and the two began a discussion; unknown to them, this would kindle a friendship. Judas had come wandering in from the small village of Bethlehem, distraught with his youth, and with what he feared was his life before him. Confident but lonely, even with Pesach and family, Judas was meandering his way through life. Hillel grew up privileged by Jewish standards and was on a path of trial-free living—and yet he was equally lonely. Judas wanted freedom from the family business of olive trees, and Hillel desperately wanted freedom from the chains that were represented by the priesthood.

While Pesach would dedicate himself to his teacher, over time Hillel and Judas would meet often and secure a bond that was nearly as uncommon as it was real. The older Hillel noted

Judas's wisdom, which far outpaced his now fourteen years. Hillel took it upon himself to work with him, albeit in the abbreviated manner that it was, hoping to impress Gamaliel. Judas actually offered a trade-off—he would help galvanize Hillel's Greek. Many a Torah was being translated into the Greek language, and Hillel was, of course, accustomed to the Hebrew, but needed to improve his Greek. Judas found his mother's lessons were paying dividends right away. The two youth were close almost immediately, though they had nothing in common save their personalities, given by God himself. To two growing young men, it was all they needed.

Whenever Judas made his way to town to visit his cousin, he would find his only friend—Hillel—and the two would catch up. Gamaliel allowed space for the relationship; Hillel had been his prize pupil of late. The last two years and nine months Hillel had dedicated to the great teacher had inspired and encouraged both men, so it was a license he gave to Hillel that he granted to few others.

Hillel's cleverness had served him well in his young years, and having a father on the Jewish ruling council did not hurt either. Though the priesthood was still a religious office, the merging with Rome had created other "priests" within the Jewish ranks—namely tax collectors and "watchmen" for the real priests. Hillel's father was one of them. It did not take long for the talk among the young men to come around to the cynicism of the day, and when it did, Hillel fully expected Judas to shy away from him once he learned his father's vocation. Judas, however, was very passive, even forgiving, of the whole matter. Hillel was relieved; he did not realize that Judas didn't dare jeopardize this budding relationship.

As with all young men who desired significance, Hillel could not resist showing his father's hand to his new friend— the secret code of payoffs among the priesthood. Judas listened intently to Hillel's details. Stories that Judas could tell, wisdom he could gain, and knowledge he could use was being freely given him. Hillel truly wanted to impress his friend, and at the same time, free himself from the burdened shoulders of a young Jewish boy.

"There is a marriage, of sorts, between the priests and the magistrates," Hillel would explain to his young apprentice. "In exchange for peace and order, the priests are given seats close to the action in local customs. More important than this, and perhaps the very reason for everything, the exchange for a peaceful people is a share in the tax revenue.

"It helped them," the young rabbi explained to Judas, "to keep our rules strict and our authority sharp, and the extra money supplemented the trade in the temple courts nicely." Now the Greek lessons were making more sense, Judas realized.

Judas also realized another important truth. *Opportunities*, he thought, *are right here in front of me.* If Judas could help Hillel with his Greek and tag along, he too could benefit from the arrangement Hillel had explained, possibly land a job, and in some way manage a career elsewhere than the family farm. His mind would race; these thoughts were a balm to his unfavorable circumstances on the farm. He could make it here; he could make a living.

In his heart, however, Judas *knew*: though he was eager, and had shown great interest in local customs, and though he possessed an astute, calculable faith and direction when it came to the Torah, he would always be returning home to work. He was certain he was entertaining fantasy, something that ought not to be done. It all amounted to naught, he reasoned with himself. His destiny would lie in farming and whatever else the business world brought him. But he would continue to meet with Hillel whenever he was allowed, and they always picked up where they had left off.

Hippicus was Judas's nickname for his friend. "Hillel the Hippicus," he would taunt, as his friend struggled with the Greek Judas was trying to bestow. This too was a salve to Judas's soul—if he could not escape his destiny, he would have fun with those who were different. The Great Herod had named a tower after his friend Hippicus, and once Judas learned that interesting fact from Hillel, it was all the fuel he needed. He visited and revisited with his friend the basics and the pronunciations of Greek, and stood proudly by as Hillel recited the language. It was Judas's project, after all, and he owned it. Not because he was a dutiful, responsible young man, but because it provided him purpose. He had found something to do, something he *could* do, and something he could be proud of. Something that was his. In many ways, Gamaliel would owe Judas for instructing his pupil! Hillel soon passed him in knowledge, but their bond had been formed, and it was strong.

Hillel's gift in return to Judas was imparting knowledge. It was through Hillel that Judas learned just how well the Jewish Council had embraced the Roman state, how embedded were the trade relationships between the magistrates and the members of the Council. These two young men had a strange marriage of sorts, one that centered not so much on a desire to mesh cultures, but a desire to extract from their friendship every drachma possible within the context of that relationship.

It was this knowledge that would serve Judas when it mattered most.

On Depression

"There is no point in treating a depressed person as though she were just feeling sad, saying, 'There now, hang on, you'll get over it.' Sadness is more or less like a head cold—with patience, it passes. Depression is like cancer."
—Barbara Kingsolver[2]

We can only guess what Judas's mind-set was, but someone who grows up on the outskirts of life can easily fall prey to an outcast mentality. Judas would certainly encounter those who would put him in his place, call into question his place among great men, and belittle him along the way. The rapidity of his ascent and descent would not necessarily lead one to deep wells of depression, but the illness is worth examining given the current trends in society, and the temptations to change our views into continually pessimistic ones.

Depression is a sad friend lurking in the corner, always there, readily saving you a seat in the shadows.

> Depression is a sad friend lurking in the corner, always there, readily saving you a seat in the shadows.

Depression is the convinced understanding that, at any given moment, *I am not like everyone else in whatever capacity is deemed necessary by society. Something about me is incomplete. Something about me makes me worth less. Something makes me seem subhuman.* It is tricky, it is situational in nature for some, neurological for some, and a mixture, at times, for others. It manifests physically, psychologically, and physiologically in its victims. It may only feel like a slighting offense at times, but it is completely stifling and debilitating at others.

When we are faced with obstacles in life, and we no longer wish to fight, there is a moment when urgency leaves and we surrender, at least for that battle. That is a seed of sadness—where we judge ourselves as failing while actually just being tired and temporarily off track. When the energy to perform a task or continue the merry-go-round of life is replaced by reasoning and excusing, that is the fuel that keeps sadness alive and building. How can this be? Because the reasoning, justifying, and excusing is all built around the knowledge that, for whatever reason, we have stopped trying. As a dear therapist friend of mine says, "We 'should' ourselves."

"I should have worked out."
"I should be eating differently."
"I should have said something when
I heard they had a hard time."
"I should have saved more money."

That reasoning quickly births excuses, and a sense of a

new reality, one with a cloud over us, is born. We could just acknowledge that it might have been good for us to do something we didn't, but people who struggle with depression compound the "shoulds" with judgment. This judgment takes over to form a new reality, one in which our normal obligations cannot be completed, because we reason that our failure at a task has made us *lesser*, or worse yet, we failed because we think we *are* lesser. Knowing we are faced with a new trajectory based on our failure, the soil in our minds becomes fertile for depression. Never mind the billions of decisions that others have faced and failed on; the depressed mind, for some reason, fixates on a failure and makes it a permanent member of the personality carrying it, something beyond just a temporary setback. The mind compounds this with other situations of failure in our personal history, and snowballs these items together to become descriptive of the entire person.

One trick depression can play is luring us into unhealthy introspection. Everyone needs a break. No one disputes that. Where we used to reward the "workaholic," we now see the need for balance. But when life is buzzing on around us, and we can't seem to fit ourselves into the mold of normal functionality, the depressed mind lets itself off the hook through a tricky release valve. We suddenly remember all the books that were going to be read, the other people we were going to spend time talking with, and more. We effectively unplug from everyday duties, while perhaps performing the bare minimum of responsibilities, in order to

> The mind compounds this with other situations of failure in our personal history, and snowballs these items together to become descriptive of the entire person.

focus on our secondary world: one of seclusion, dissociation, and detachment. Suddenly there is another world discovered that has been stored in the mind all along—a comfort zone of sorts, complete with all the trappings needed to keep its occupant right there. Once inside, making mistakes that we convince ourselves no one can know about, the downward spiral gains speed. Healthy people take time to unplug, rest, and recuperate. Those of us who have struggled with depression know the feeling of wanting to take a break from *life itself*: a leave of absence where we knowingly retreat in hopes of finding sleep, another self, or, in the darkest moments, death itself. We sustain an existence where we act the part but are actually embedded in another world.

For some people, depression is literally wired into the brain. Most "normal" functioning people do not like to hear that. Indeed, I have been in fellowships of churches that simply "spiritualize" the entire thing! "There must be something wrong with you spiritually"; or, "Perhaps there is something you need to confess, to explain why you're down." Since few are adequately equipped to deal with things of this nature, particularly where internal rewiring (as much as possible) takes months and likely years, people of faith can drop back and find reasons to avoid their friend's pain rather than embrace the struggling person and seek to understand.

Given the dichotomy of the depressed mind, what most people don't realize is how amazingly talented many depressed members of society are. After all, bills get paid, promotions happen, love and marriage exist, children are pro-created—life beats on in the depressed state for millions of people, every day, worldwide. For instance, how impressive is the mind that cannot bear itself and yet finds a way to soldier on and look quite normal! Even with all the activity, the decaying heart of the depressed person can often *look* alive and well. The busyness of their life is juxtaposed against the person inside, who battles internally. It is hard, tiring work for a person to live in two realities, and yet that is the dilemma faced by one living with depression—a life where we must function, and another where we don't want to.

Is There No 'Off Switch'?

So what is this life like for one struggling with the chains of depression? Society's expectations are burdensome for many—even without a triggering trauma event. Consider the relatively newly coined term *seasonal affective disorder,* named in the 1980s by Norman Rosenthal and others. This is indeed a very real phenomenon, one affecting many people in most circles of society. And yet, while there is relief when a friend or professional can put a finger on how we are feeling during a given season, and provide descriptions of symptoms—and we say, "That's exactly how I feel!"—do we ever stop to wonder what causes this phenomenon? Do many people get blue in the late fall and winter? Perhaps. Now consider this: in many countries, especially developed countries, people are expected to function at the *same level of busyness* all twelve months of the year. We are expected to run, jump, and play. And shop. And work. And spend—all year round, all the time. If we aren't "on" all year, well, there must be something wrong, right? Perhaps. And yet perhaps we are supposed to take time to reflect, to write, to read, to rest, or maybe just to find a favorite blanket—and not run ourselves ragged all the time. So while disorders are real, and can spark bouts of sadness and lead to depressive states, it's also true that as humans on planet earth we can fall victim to our own expectations.

In eras past, when humans were hunter-gatherers, or predominantly agrarian or tradesmen, we had seasons of life, rest, and extreme activity. Of course, the lack of electricity didn't hurt either. Now workout gyms are open twenty-four hours a day, seven days a week, 365 days a year. Stores are open all night, all throughout the holidays, and there are three shifts to a working day. People are always supposed to be "on"—no "off" switch is allowed. If a person isn't acclimated to this kind of constant activity, he or she can easily develop symptoms of depression. The only real "out" of this societal rut is to be comfortable with being different from most of what culture tells us we need to be. That is a gift any individual can give himself or herself: the ability to accept being different and "untrendy" when it matters most—for a person's mental well-being. Our activity doesn't need to be predicated on whether something is the "right thing to do." After all, haven't we learned that society often—maybe usually—doesn't have the right answers?

Those who have gone down depressed roads—biological, situational, or otherwise—must grapple with the eventual trajectory of facing death through this rut. Perhaps they also—knowingly or not—find themselves pushing hard toward that end.

Many people provide warning signals. They might hint or

drop an "I wish it could be over" clue, but most of us are too busy trying to keep up with our own lives to take these warning bells seriously. If we aren't too busy, we're too skeptical to understand that some people do not have the ability to digest and reconcile their feelings with the life around them, and we fail to see that their only attempts at popping up their periscope for help are too often met with denial—or even worse—laughter. To be brave enough to admit depression is important; telling someone you have had thoughts of ending your life is even braver. It is also a necessary and perhaps lifesaving relief valve to suspend your mind's train of thought until you can spend greater time walking your thoughts out with someone who will listen.

Many people I talk with really don't want to hear about depression. They equate their feelings of sadness about their favorite team losing with someone who suffers from a "glass-half empty" life, without understanding that the depressed person likely faces brain chemistry or other physiological/psychological issues. Since many cannot understand the issues, we blow them off or ignore the possible consequences—sometimes until it's too late. A popular phrase these days is "checking in" with a trusted friend. This works, but once the check-in is done, there needs to be loving follow-up, more listening, serious conversation, and usually counseling, very possibly with the need for medication. Make no mistake: being sad about an event or events is far different than being caught in the deep pits of depression.

Many of us face stress-induced panic episodes, depression-based thought patterns, and self-deprecating thinking. Unknown to us, there are many pitfalls we can fall into that can spiral out of control—even ruin our day-to-day outlook. I will never forget making a mistake on a job and saying "I'm an idiot" under my breath, berating myself for doing something so elementary in such an incorrect manner. Only to hear my boss sternly correct me: "Don't be so hard on yourself." That is just one moment from fifteen years ago. It was a helpful correction, though, as I wasn't even aware I was entertaining such defeating self-talk. I would saunter on for many years, unaware I was under my own cloud before taking steps to do something about it.

There are no easy answers to depression. But the recognition of the rut we can get our minds into is a start. It can be difficult just to answer a most basic question: What is considered "normal" thinking anyway? To a child brought up with abuse, poking siblings with knives can be considered normal if no blood is drawn! We all have different backgrounds, circumstances, and experiences that make up our levels of cognition. The more we speak to others, particularly those around us who are older, more experienced, or more educated, the more we can find answers to our questions and much-needed perspective.

> There are no easy answers to depression. But the recognition of the rut we can get our minds into is a start.

When we try and measure ourselves by others—whether by career, lifestyle, or general busyness—without the understanding that these other people are not our standard, it is a recipe for disaster. Others are not our scorecards. If we have to wrestle with our own thoughts and humanity, and simultaneously measure up to our peers, it is exhausting. However, as said earlier, depressed people are unusually talented in walking this line.

Many of us have been sad, and many of us have had seasons of depression. Job transitions, going off-duty from military service, postpartum depression—the list goes on. Some who suffer don't realize it; they just think they're grumpy. Again, we are cultured and trained to perform, and taking the time to ask ourselves if we're really happy can seem like a "stupid mental exercise." Having difficulty facing life's challenges isn't a disease; it's normal.

Facing our depression head-on takes more guts than ignoring it and trudging on. Perhaps it's time to get open with those in our circle. Or perhaps we need to make some changes to those who are within our circle!

Beth

Beth is a good friend. My wife and I treasure our relationship with her and her family. The funny thing is, describing Beth as being part of a family is a huge part of her story. She grew up understanding that depression follows her family line. Many people who deal with depression process that reality differently. Beth's father processed his reality with alcohol. Her parents divorced when she was young, and her father was scarcely present. She shares that the physical manifestations of her depression include waking and not being able to return to sleep, being sad for no apparent reason, possessing little or no motivation, and being consistently tired, as if just having run a marathon. Given that scorecard as a start, Beth nevertheless walked through most of her adult life dealing with the beast that is depression medicine-free. After all, there are always fears of side effects and changes to a person's personality once medicine is introduced. Beth is a Christian, and she relied on her faith and counseling to assist her battle, and checked off all the societal boxes in the face of her obstacles. That is talent.

In spite of these hurdles, Beth boldly advanced and today is married with a wonderful life in front of her, pressing upward in her field with degrees and amazing work environments. She and her husband were living the dream, so to speak, in their suburban home, with their careers and their degrees and their cat. Then one day . . . Beth got pregnant. It's safe to say this wasn't part of the plan. Beth was well outside the normal age range for childbearing, but a miracle is a miracle, right? Either way, pregnancy was upon her and her husband, and it brought about a myriad of changes to her mind and body. As any mother can attest, the transformation is both beautiful and scary. A certain smoothness of skin is replaced by an outer layer with a something like a reptilian hardness, body dimensions change, hormones are intensely affected—the list goes on.

But Beth had an additional set of reactions. Just before she gave birth, she realized some of her cloud of depression was caused by sexual abuse within her family. Repressed through all the years but silently following her, the memory reared its ugly head at the most inopportune time.

Within a couple days of giving birth, severe anxiety began to taunt her. It was ferocious. She would lament the day she was born. She would rue the very birth of her daughter. Her beautiful mind, positive and dignified, now entertained thoughts of giving her child up; she wanted her old life back. As she would confide, "This little being was attached like a leech, and I couldn't break free or separate from it." Beth was in a very dark place, becoming something and someone she could scarcely recognize. Postpartum depression is much darker even than normal depression, she would say. Thoughts of suicide and even ways to kill her offspring would haunt her during her darkest episodes. So many hormones for a woman to go through—carrying a little being and birthing a child into the world is so much more than a nine-month workout. It is a truly transformative, permanent part of a woman, and Beth felt it clearly: she seemed to be rejecting this massive change. There was nothing she could do to regain her now former life.

There were long months of sleepless nights, now coupled with a crying baby and racked nerves of new parenting, before she could "return to her baseline," as she calls it—where she knew the score and was comfortable with her par values. Today, she is coping in progressive ways with her self-talk, not comparing herself to others' scorecards, and entirely comfortable with who she is. She would revive her life by reciting Scripture, seeing a psychiatrist who would help her get the right combination of medicine, and finding a couple of counselors to help her walk her new avenue in life.

She has come a long way—from the depths of despair to a position where she knows that what she experienced was meant for her growth, and to develop the ability to help others who may deal with similar paths. She is the radiant person she once was, but now with a bit more knowledge, a bit more peace, and a lot more wisdom.

Do you face a hovering cloud? Is it difficult to get through tough times when others don't seem to be facing problems? It will serve us well to determine the things needed for our own good. We may be missing out on the best of ourselves, and others may be missing out as well. Either way, depression is not something to be taken lightly, ignored, or allowed to fester. Take the time; talk with others through life. It's not weakness to do a close assessment of ourselves or admit we aren't comfortable with society's values on important matters like the use of time and energy. We may hold the keys to our own happiness after all.

> Take the time; talk with others through life. It's not weakness to do a close assessment of ourselves.

VACATION

As a young man growing up in the shadow of work and carrying the anchor of younger siblings, Judas grew more and more at odds with his circumstances. It was not merely a short-lived attitude problem; it was one of life placement. Judas was certain he was being left out of life. Something inside him was increasingly discontented by a life farming an olive grove. Perhaps it was the distant murmurings from Jerusalem or the flicker of her candlelight on clear evenings. Judas would wander the hills outside Bethlehem, kicking stones—and his future—around. The thought world of a young man on a hillside in the evening is the material of poets and sages; this constant peering toward Jerusalem took its toll on Judas. He wanted out.

Then a window of opportunity arrived. The summer he turned sixteen, prior to the busy harvest season, Judas was given permission to stay a full three months with his cousin Pesach. The boys had spent much time with one another through the years, growing up together through it all. Pesach's father, Lemil, had passed when the boys were young. But Pesach had a special uncle in Simon, who would see to his sister's needs, and a friend of sorts in Judas, who neither judged nor pitied him. Their family ties were tight, and now they represented Judas's great glimmer of hope and escape.

It was a great respite from life, and a chance for Judas to spread his wings. To a sixteen-year-old used to being attached to the duties of a family unit, this was a great revelation—a test, a taste of what might lie in his future. Manhood was calling him, and a city like Jerusalem provided all the adventure he needed. And this time away would not be for a mere few weeks, but practically his entire summer.

The years of labor had trained his body; he was up habitually early every morning. Like most young men in his culture, he had little fat to speak of and was as wiry as they come. His days spent climbing had chiseled his frame to such a degree it was as if he were training to compete in the Games. This labor and discipline sculpted him. Now, being away from home and having nothing calling him—no father, no grove, no serving the little ones—Judas was finally free. During this time he would venture eagerly out to the northern hill, called Scopus, where he would meditate and pray. Though not a focused, driven, spiritual Jew, he did spend time with his God, and now that time was even more precious to his searching soul.

It was quite an advantage that his cousin lived close to the mount, though there were several to choose from. Judas's home was nothing but fields in practically every direction, so he welcomed this new view. He felt closer to God here, maybe because Judas felt as though he saw things from God's perspective while in this place. Everything was quieter, more distant, more peaceful. It was here that he vented to God about his circumstances, though, in truth, this is a frequent sixteen-

> At sixteen, Judas felt he was ripe for his own quest for significance.

year-old complaint, not one exclusive to Judas. The age of significance for men begins, perhaps, in their middle teenage years. At sixteen, Judas felt he was ripe for his own quest for significance. It was during the early mornings, when society below these hills was first waking, when the animals were rising, and the sun beginning to feed the earth, that his ambition was unimpeded; he could dream. The trouble was, Judas wasn't sure what to dream about.

The simple truth was that Judas was sick of the olive business. One minute he would rejoice to his God about his freedom and the relief he felt during this vacation, and then he would turn to a time of pleading for escape from the only life he had known. He was lost in his heart, having missed the only real opportunity for a young man in the Jewish community (though he was still not sold in his heart on the priesthood). He was rueful of the fact that he was subject to a family business and eventual inheritance in which he had no interest. He had his entire life before him—and he was dreading it.

As with many his age, his attention span was only so long. There were countless things to do in the bustling city below, and Judas couldn't wait to get started. Inside, the call of life was strong, but Judas managed to stuff it all away in an attempt to simply enjoy his summer.

His angst would have to wait. Pesach and he had a myriad of things to see and do within the walls of the great city. They would map it out and conquer each of her streets in turn. It made for a conquest of sorts, and their minds were filled with each day, each sight, and each adventure. Amid the tradition that was the City of David—while dismissing what it perhaps was becoming—they released themselves to enjoy what men and women were capable of enjoying: the creating, displaying, and selling of wares.

It was a Friday. Friday was the day for market. On this particular day, Pesach's mother sent the two of them to buy her more of the beads she would use to, in Pesach's words, "waste her time in creativity." It was a bittersweet day: the two young men had a day to explore the pagan-filled marketplace, but it was Friday, so they needed to be home in time to bathe and prepare for the Sabbath. A wise aunt curtails behavior where and when she can, and Pesach's mother knew the best way to get the young men away from the social atrocities of the market was to send them there on a Friday. They were a devout family guided by the deep faith of this widow. Judas's aunt held a formal dinner to begin the Sabbath ritual, so she employed her boys as errand runners.

Judas and Pesach were making their way through Jerusalem's market, hurrying to see what they could while, at the same time, trying to drink it all in as slowly as possible. There was plenty of corruption in this place. Many areas of the Holy City had become as morally depraved as the usual environs surrounding their captors. And though it was the Holy City, paganism was strong: many emblems, idols, and prayer beads were for sale; in some cases, so were the people who tried to sell them. When it came down to it, pretty much everything was for sale or some type of barter in the marketplace. And for the two young men, it also meant this: no real regulations facing them meant new adventures, and with the license to be in this place given by Judas's Aunt Rama herself, time and conscience were their only constraints.

This Friday afternoon was different, however. As they

strolled through one last market stall, there was a small crowd just outside it, harassing the local cripple. The man had some defect; his legs were shriveled. They were small in comparison with other grown men, but it was difficult to tell initially; he covered himself with a partially ribbed blanket from the waist down. His only luggage was a small bundle which probably had inside it a separate tunic or perhaps another blanket for when night fell. He had a small, round bowl made of hemp that he held up with shaky hands, asking for any spare coins the passing crowds might not mind parting with. Dirt was all over him, and Judas remarked to his cousin that the man's nails made it look as though he had been working in an olive grove for a month.

He was a constant presence in this area and, to most, a constant nuisance. The man running the adjacent store would kick him repeatedly in vain attempts to shoo him away. He didn't want people like this man cluttering up his market area. Cripples like him took away money before it could enter his store. Both Judas and his cousin found the scene amusing. They stood watching the "free circus," as Judas liked to call it.

One who appeared to be a leader, average in stature, smiled a bit, and turned to finish whatever he was saying to the group following him.

As they began to make their way out, a group of people came around the corner—slowly, yet deliberately. One who appeared to be a leader, average in stature, smiled a bit, and turned to finish whatever he was saying to the group following him. It appeared to Judas to be just another rabbi, though this one did seem to have a larger flock. There were actually a few women also, who followed along in the back. This seemed strange if not immodest or even borderline indecent. This was highly unusual, and it caught the attention of both young men.

It was customary for the rabbis to rotate their duties from one province or borough to another. There was a fleecing, as it were, of each other's areas; the purpose was to find the best candidates to train in the faith. It was a still a delicate matter—largely because the priests and local magistrate demanded they maintain some semblance of communication even in their travels. The high priest for the year, however, would leave the searching and vetting of candidates to the younger representatives of the sect. "This one must have been one of the younger rabbis from another borough," Pesach said to Judas. "But why are these women following him too?"

The rabbi stopped and spoke briefly with the beggar, who cowered at first. "What a strange thing," Judas thought aloud, though only Pesach could hear him. "Who would cower from a rabbi? What business would a rabbi have with a cripple anyway, except to display to his pupils the curse that must be present?" It made no sense, nor did it seem to fit that the rabbi had no flowing robe, nor did he have scribes to carry his scrolls, take names, or record what was spoken. As they looked closer, Judas and his cousin saw he had no scrolls at all. Perhaps he wasn't a rabbi after all, Judas thought, though in many respects, this man spoke like one. They overheard him quoting Scripture and teaching his group after speaking with the cripple.

Then Judas saw him do something that proved he was no rabbi—he reached out and touched the unclean man's hand. The beggar looked up at him, not entirely unlike a maiden looking into the eyes of a suitor. There was murmuring and some gasping from the crowd. The man put his hand over the beggar's hands, closed his eyes, and appeared to pray. Then he stopped, and the beggar yanked his hands back, as if suddenly offended. Then the cripple slowly turned his head, his eyes moving toward his lifeless legs. He took his hands and cautiously gripped his blanket. With one swift yank, he uncovered his lower body. The crowd that followed the teacher engulfed the man, clouding the boys' line of sight. What they *did* see was the crowd stepping back and gasping, almost in unison. What Judas saw next was an image he would never forget—the once crippled man standing in the middle of the crowd. Both Judas and his cousin had been staring at this scene the entire time, and they now found themselves walking briskly toward the crowd.

One man had fought his way out of the crowd and was running headlong down the road, past the boys, shouting something about a miracle. There was a large commotion brewing, and the storekeeper emerged, waving a stick and yelling at them all to leave. Dust was flying up everywhere. The keeper took the stick and hit the healed cripple hard across his back, knocking him over, muttering something along the lines of "fraud." As Judas and Pesach began to leave, the now healed beggar was standing, weeping, and praising God. The rabbi turned, spoke to the crowd—saying something the boys could not entirely make out, something about the power of God—and walked on.

Judas hit his cousin in the arm—harder than he meant to. *"Did you see that?"*

"See what?" Pesach was already annoyed. "You need to get out of the grove more, Judas. Nonsense walks these streets daily. Get a grip on yourself before you embarrass the both of us."

"No, did you *see* that? That cripple is walking now. He wasn't before. And did you see the way the rabbi touched him? What's with that?"

Pesach looked incredulously at his cousin. "You're not serious, are you? Look, we need to get back. Mother's bound to be ready for us, and we'll both hear about it if we're late. It was just another setup to get money. The best way to tell the real rabbis from the fakes is to see who follows them—and how large their money pouch is. Open up your eyes, will ya?"

"Maybe you're just cynical." It was a simple retort from Judas, but an honest one.

Pesach stopped abruptly. "Judas, you know so little of the way things are here. You think you know, but you have no idea. People around here will rob you blind if you're not careful. You need to stick with me if you want to keep your money." He laughed and now it was his turn to punch his cousin. Pesach frequently and easily amused himself by watching the naiveté of his cousin. Judas had come across as tough, hardened by labor and the wisdom it provided. This little incident revealed the boy still inside of the man, the dreamer who hadn't lost his sense of wonder. Pesach pounced on it.

"This place will eat you alive. People get ripped off constantly—let alone when thugs get ahold of you. What we just saw was a circus act, and you fell for it. Luckily, they didn't have time to ask you for any of your money. We might have gone home broke!" Pesach burst out laughing, finding great humor at his cousin's expense.

Maybe he is right, Judas thought.

But still, it didn't add up. He was sure of what he saw.

FROM CURIOSITY
TO DESTINY

Once they made it to Pesach's, talk shifted from the teasing streetwise cousin to more spiritual matters. It was the eve of the Sabbath, and the talk was of God, of the great things He had done, His miracles of parting the Sea, freeing the Israelites, saving Daniel . . . these were stories they had heard countless times.

Stories.

Still, Judas could not get what he had witnessed out of his mind. He tried to explain it to his aunt, as did his cousin, but to no avail. Pesach's recounting was quite different from Judas's—he added sarcasm and realism to it, details that Judas didn't appreciate. After she listened intently, they awaited the judgment of Pesach's mother. "The followers of that man must have set it up beforehand," she would explain, "so he could gain followers and do what all teachers do: make money off their followers."

"There is only One who could do such miracles," Aunt Rama continued. "And it is not someone of this world, it is the Messiah alone." She paused in her chopping of the carrots she had received from the boys. "And He has not yet come." To her and Pesach, the matter was closed.

The reasoning was clear to Judas's aunt and cousin. Why would God, who can move mountains and part seas, waste his time healing a cripple when the whole nation needed saved? Why would any self-respecting Jew give such a man the time of day? "This was the reason for the people's apostasy," his aunt would offer. "Jews meddling with trifling matters when they should be more concerned for their nation." For reasons unknown, the discussion turned down a testy path, and Judas could tell that pressing the matter would make for an uncomfortable Sabbath. And that was not a good thing for a houseguest to bring about.

The thoughts would linger for Judas. He could not forget what he saw. He would venture again into the public square, into the markets, even the temple. After all, if what he saw was true, one would think that, sooner or later, the man would be back at the synagogue.

There were still routines to tend to, even when not on a farm, and try as they might, the boys could not escape. There was dusting of drapery, sweeping of the walk in front of the home, even repair of the cheap palm roof that protected Aunt Rama's family. He kept in mind that there was no uncle to help his aunt, so he was determined to help all he could. But this did not keep Judas's mind—and body—from wandering, and every opportunity he had would be spent searching for this most unusual man and his followers.

He felt strange, seeing what he had. The knowledge that his cousin saw the same thing, but didn't afford it the same meaning, began to put a wall between them. It was as if Judas was coming alive as a man. All of the stories, the rituals, the traditions, the legends—and the guilt—were coming alive at the same time. In his eyes his faith was no longer simply a matter of intellectual belief, but becoming *actual* faith. What was dormant was being awakened. It was also scary since he was alone in this journey. His cousin refused to join him, so Judas was indeed becoming his own man. He would seek validation, and he would need it from the source—that man, the priest (he assumed he was some kind of priest) who did the unthinkable.

> The knowledge that his cousin saw the same thing, but didn't afford it the same meaning, began to put a wall between them.

Toward the end of that summer, Judas would meet him, in a manner of speaking. He had ventured alone to the marketplace. There was a large crowd in the area, and Judas somehow knew this was because of the man. He no longer thought of him as a rabbi or priest, but as a man with some gift—perhaps a magician or mystic. Whatever he had, or whoever he was, Judas would seize his opportunity and find out.

Judas began to move forward politely enough: excusing himself, lightly tapping shoulders as he made his way between people, all of whom were also vying to catch a glimpse of this miracle man. The crowd was strangely silent and attentive. The man was also, apparently, a man of wisdom, and this was a day of teaching. The crowd was large, but Judas finally made it close enough to hear his voice and see the top of the man's head. It was as close as he could get without forcing his way through people, so he stopped.

The speech was one he would never forget, and it spoke to Judas in a voice that seemed to come from within. When the priests and rabbis would come through town, they were, to Judas, a group of men who swept away his friends. In truth, and in his heart, they swept away his future. Priests sought to tell young men like Judas what they could not be; they drew limitations instead of giving choices.

They came, he thought, as royalty unto themselves, as men with servants and slaves who were learning to be like them. Their scribes, their servants, all reminded Judas of the slaves and bondservants he had seen rich men possess. It was absurd to him that these men, whose life's definition was to serve God, were scouring the streets looking for more youth to serve themselves— and to be trained to do the same. As he remembered this, he realized, for the first time, that it was not a desire to be far from God that he possessed, but a desire not to be a servant of men. Judas hated his religion, but wanted to love God.

> Priests sought to tell young men like Judas what they could not be; they drew limitations instead of giving choices.

What the miracle worker was saying that day spoke directly to his heart. He spoke not of his own power; he spoke of hypocrisy. "Men disfigure their faces to show they are fasting; they make a big showing of their prayers and wear long, flowing robes, all to be seen by others." *Exactly*, Judas thought. He phrased it precisely how Judas would. Now it was not just a miracle Judas wanted an explanation for; it was the man's mind that Judas wanted to understand.

He pressed a bit harder on the man in front of him, until

the man pushed back a bit. Then Judas figured a plan: the best way was to go down—low. So what if he could not see him for a short time, he thought. He risked making a ruckus for the opportunity to see this man face to face. He would crawl.

And it worked. Within just a few moments, a few bumps, a couple of stepped-on fingers, he had made it through the crowd. Judas popped up, right in front of the man—completely covered in dust—and stood facing him. He felt fairly stupid at first, dusting himself off, feeling fear and embarrassment, as though he did not want to be noticed for what he had done. And then an amazing thing happened: the man stopped his speaking, looked at young Judas, smiled for a second . . . and then the smile disappeared. He continued a discourse about being void of self and embracing the purposes of God for humankind, not just for the glorification of the Jewish nation.

Once the man had completed his talk, he stepped down from the stump he had been standing on and began to walk on. Judas simply followed. He wasn't walking with the crowd, he wasn't even walking with this man, the one he heard them call Jesus. He was following something he had never encountered before. He was following the one thing, or person, that had eluded him his entire young life. He was following truth. He was following courage.

As he walked, he was straining to hear through the crowd, trying to make sense of everything the man said. They seemed to make little progress down the road. Jesus stopped frequently, sometimes of his choice and others due to the wishes of those around him. Some worked their way almost violently through the crowds, carrying with them various children, beggars, crippled, and the like. Once they reached Jesus, the hurrying came to a halt, and time itself seemed to stand still. Jesus was living and explaining the life of God, and everywhere he walked it was as if a sort of divinity reigned.

Not all of the teaching was new; there were actually many great orators and speakers of the day. But most would finish a talk, which was always previously prepared, deliver some type of humor, and fade away, within a short time, to another town or borough. Jesus did not seem to provide much humor. Nor did he seem to come prepared with speeches. Yet he *was* prepared. Completely. He was serious, like a rabbi, but serene, like Judas's mother. It was a strange calm, Judas would note, and a strange sensation of peace he had not felt since he was a boy. It was this feeling that kept drifting back into his psyche, even as Jesus was teaching, talking, and praying. Judas had to squint his eyes and shake his head for a second or two, just to snap out of the trance he found himself in. This Jesus was not hypnotizing people, but Judas could not shake the feeling he had in his presence. It was genuine authority.

> He was serious, like a rabbi, but serene, like Judas's mother. It was a strange calm, Judas would note, and a strange sensation of peace he had not felt since he was a boy.

As the day was drawing to a close, Judas had to tear himself away from the crowd, as did most of the others, and find his way back, through several blocks of homes and shops, out of the city, and to his aunt's house. Judas was familiar enough with the area, but the time with Jesus had him noticing less where he was and more of what he had been hearing. It took him a few minutes to find his bearings and out of the city. Off he went, leaving Jesus, jubilant and yet somehow, in some way, more confused.

As he walked, he began to digest not only what he had heard and seen from Jesus but also from the people he had spoken with as they walked. There were the gazers, those who were mystified still, who did not seem to get beyond the prayers and the presence. There were other men, who would repeat or speak some of the same statements over and over, as if to commit them to memory. And there were countless others who would listen for a time and walk on, unimpressed.

This time with Jesus had confirmed upon Judas what he hoped: he was not crazy. He now really believed what he had seen. It wasn't because Jesus had healed, but because his words and wisdom matched his actions. So what was Judas to do about his discovery? He thought it necessary to do *something*. For the first time in his young life, he felt the urge to act. He just didn't know exactly what that meant.

> For the first time in his young life, he felt the urge to act. He just didn't know exactly what that meant.

His thoughts turned to the men who walked closest to Jesus: his students. There was a group even within the group who seemed to marvel at the man a little less than others—if that were possible —and Judas decided that it was from this group that he could discern where Jesus would be in the morning. Judas admired these men, but was dismayed. Something had been ignited in him; he had seemed to find his own heart. He realized as he walked that he wanted to know this God—*his* God. It was this God whom Judas wanted to serve; not this religion. He had found a teacher who was not a rabbi, but at the same time was better than a rabbi—a man who paid him some mind, if even for a moment.

His newest disappointment, however, was with the men who had indicated Jesus' location. They must have been his chosen, Judas thought. Judas was on the outside looking in yet again. This time not from the hilltop of Bethlehem, removed from the life of the city, but in a distant country in his mind. Jesus could have been a million miles away or just over a wall, but to Judas it was a recurring theme: he was shut out again, and the olive grove would just keep growing. He had been passed over yet again—not by being on the outside of a chosen group, but by destiny. Jesus had picked his men, his disciples, and Judas was too late. It was his fate, Judas thought. Again.

Still, he could not get enough of the man. Pesach had more or less been forbidden by his protective mother, but Judas was free to go. There was something happening in their house, and Judas could not quite put his finger on it. But at the same time it was clear enough: Pesach's mother was "protecting" her son. In reality, she was protecting herself from her own fears. She needed her son home, not out following some circus—or, worse, swept into some crusade that would see him imprisoned or beheaded.

So Judas took his liberty well and, for once, felt thankful he was trusted by his father to be where he was.

The next day was a bit more challenging. Judas had gone to the place the other young men had mentioned as a point of connection, but it was void of any activity save a few grumbling old men. *Did they lie to me?* he thought of the ones he had asked the previous day. Or had he been late because of the morning chores from his aunt? He was immediately restless, as though he was rowing upstream again; fate was trying to deal him another blow. But he made haste, having been told by one of the men that the throng had made its way toward the Upper City.

Judas ran.

He was missing out, and he knew it. When he finally reached the crowd, it was even larger than the day before. The teaching for the day, he was told, centered on blessings from God, that there was a special treasure to be had if people were meek, humble, and sought after God. Jesus mentioned on more than one occasion the need to follow him, which was strange, because most rabbis had men seeking them, and had to pick and choose the best. This man had throngs after him, but seemed to give thinning statements as he went, ones that talked about how difficult it was to follow him. It was all so very confusing. After a while, Judas learned a valuable lesson: to follow this man was to stop comparing him to what he knew of the common teachers.

> After a while, Judas learned a valuable lesson: to follow this man was to stop comparing him to what he knew of the common teachers.

Judas began rising earlier in the day; his vacation was nearly over. His chores were done well, as usual, but hurriedly, so as to meet up with Jesus and his men as quickly as possible. The late summer heat was sizzling, the air dry. Dust engulfed them wherever they went; the crowd was thick, food and water scarce. No matter: the energy level never ceased. There was a sort of drinking in taking place among the crowd: not of water but of divine guidance, wisdom, and love. Mixed in, as they walked, were men speaking of the fulfillment of Scripture, and arguments would break out as soon as Jesus left.

Judas seemed to look at Scripture anew. The minimal number of scrolls in Aunt Rama's house now read differently than they had before; if he were honest, he had barely picked them up before all this. Now, however, Judas would not part with them. Though he was actually more fluent in Greek, he understood enough of the native language to see, and eagerness did the rest. Late at night, while his cousin slept, Judas was up, reading by dim candlelight. He had found something for himself, and in Scripture he learned a different way. Inside, he saw a new God, one who created out of love, disciplined out of love, and cried at His people's faults. Genesis was no longer about a distant Creator God, but a father with soft eyes and a warm heart.

It was now one week before Judas was to return to the grove. He had spent the better part of five weeks following around this man Jesus, as had countless others. Judas had begun to arrive first thing after daybreak, and he was eager to learn and be with the others. Daily teaching, encouragement, and the warmest smile that accompanied them were the gifts for those who heard. Judas was fueled by it, more than he would have liked to admit, though he tried his best to take an impartial observer's stance. He wanted to drink in as much as he could before his vacation ended and reality returned.

It was one of Judas's final days in Jerusalem. Jesus took a group of about thirty or so, walked in a direct path outside the town, and headed toward the top of the Mount of Olives. They were over on the southern side now and had cleared the city gate. He didn't stop for anyone, not even a pause for the poor who gathered at the gate. *Strange*, all the people thought. Maybe this was it; maybe the ministry was over. Maybe he had finally gotten kicked out.

It was not uncommon for centurions to do the dirty biddings of their magistrates at night. Plenty of movements were squashed with the leaders being taken at night from their home, or wherever they stayed. Their followers would gather the next day to see their leader strung up, hear of his arrest, or listen to more invigorating messages—and many times found *themselves* under arrest. Perhaps Jesus had stirred up too much concern and, out of deference to the crowds, the Romans were simply shipping him out.

The crowd followed him, but the people looked behind themselves quite a bit. There were plenty of rumblings. After all, the crowds were rather bothersome even in the bustle of the city. Everyone knew in the back of their minds that the authorities, be they Roman or Jewish, wouldn't stand much longer for these crowds to be gathered as frequently as they were. Though their confidence would grow at times, the imminent threat still made the followers nervous. Perhaps they had been forced to simply begin meeting in the countryside.

Whatever it was, Judas was glad he arrived early that day. One extra chore, one day of sleeping a bit later, and there was no way he would have caught them, no way he would have known to set out into the country. He felt fortunate.

Once they reached a large rock, Jesus turned to his followers and instructed them to sit and rest. He appeared to be significantly more tired than he had over the last several weeks. It looked like he hadn't eaten in a week. Jesus had tears in his eyes, and he spoke to everyone and explained that he needed to choose from among the people several who he would train on a more personal basis, several stewards of

> He needed to choose from among the people several who he would train.

his words.

And so he began listing the names and smiling at each of them. One by one, they heard their names, and they too smiled.

Judas was looking at the men Jesus had called. A couple of them were smiling almost knowingly. A couple had looks of astonishment. All were elated. Judas smiled a bit. He was happy for them, and a bit envious. He did not know if this is how the rabbis did it, but now he was seeing it for himself. Up close and personal, he was being passed over again, not because he was lost somewhere in a row of olive trees while being lectured by his father, but simply because he was not good enough. He wondered if he would have been chosen had he been there when this man Jesus began his work. Now he knew. He would not.

And then something he did not expect happened.

Judas heard his Jesus call his name.

THE CHOSEN

Everything seemed to happen so fast. Once he dismissed the remaining twenty or so back to town, Jesus turned back to the men, twelve in number, and began speaking to them. He told them they were the ones. They would be his students, his pupils, his disciples, his instruments—the ones chosen by his Father. There was much to do, and so much to be taught throughout the Jewish land. They would be given power to preach, teach, and heal in his name and under his authority.

It was exciting, but it was easy to see that not everyone believed him. He just kept on, undaunted. Jesus knew the men were too excited to comprehend what he was saying. They were still in too much shock to care about their new powers, mission, or tutelage.

Judas was trying to listen, trying to collect his mind, trying to think. *What about my family, my obligations? What about my mother and father worrying about me?* Would they be proud because he had been chosen or ashamed because this Jesus was obviously not official? What about the grove? *That stupid grove. Such an annoyance.* So much to do, so little reward. Yet it also pained him to think of his father: slaving away, and now practically alone.

It was so hard to concentrate on what Jesus was saying. He smiled a lot. He must have known Judas's thoughts, and Judas must not have been the only one, because Jesus told them to walk with him some, trust in God, and that they would begin to take on one thing at a time.

It would be a familiar sight over the next couple of years, these men walking with Jesus. At first they scrambled, trying to get close to him, close to the teaching, close to his thoughts. Though they were excited, they also seemed to forget that the crowd was gone. It was simply them who Jesus was focused on. Though he paid attention to all the people around him, at times the twelve seemed to forget that they had been specially chosen. In time, however, each of the men settled into their respective places, and an incredible sense of security engulfed them. The human tendency to clamor for position was evident, but the leadership displayed by Jesus simmered that ambition quite significantly. Some of them took longer to realize this than others, but for Judas the recognition seemed instantaneous. Perhaps it was his youth, or the instinctive training of a dominant father figure, but he found himself clinging to the security he found

> He was at once grateful and disbelieving. He needed convincing that he should be there at all.

in Jesus to quell the crushing insecurity he felt almost every minute.

He was at once grateful and disbelieving. He needed convincing that he should be there at all. He had to convince himself he belonged. Some of these men were natural leaders, boisterous even, and others wise and outspoken. Some men had left careers to join this group, and they made sure others knew about it, much to Jesus' consternation. And then there was Judas, young and unaccomplished save his ambition. It was easy for Judas to resign himself to the rear gallery of the twelve.

Simon, Andrew, James, and John were fishermen. Fishermen tell tales, and these men were no different. One would think by the way they talked that Jerusalem and the surrounding area would not survive without their businesses. Others, in Judas's eyes, were forgetful of their pasts. So Judas, in a natural sort of way, ended up spending most of his time with Matthew, the tax collector.

The two spoke of the Jewish customs and what Judas had gleaned in his time with Hillel. Matthew was all too accustomed to the topic, having spent his life procuring his security from his fellow Jews. It was a dangerous mix, these hardworking men with their own businesses—men who by nature grumbled at the prospect of giving up monies to those who had not worked to earn anything—now finding themselves in company with a collector of taxes and tolls. Though Matthew was repentant, nothing about his presence proved an easy pill to swallow. It would be a sore subject, sometimes spoken of and sometimes not. Judas for one, however, understood the value of the Jew who could adapt to the local customs and

Roman rule.

Judas would find himself in the middle of these conversations—and sometimes confrontations—between Peter and the others with Matthew. If it were not for Jesus, on more than one occasion these men may have come to blows. Matthew had done a complete turnaround—and this was known to most of the men—prior to being chosen to be among the twelve. He had openly confessed taking monies far in excess of the Roman tax code. This was a confirmation—and a permanent labeling—to all who heard. Matthew had taken advantage of his fellow Jews, and that was sin upon sin. It was one thing to collect taxes for Rome against your people; it was quite another to add extortion or embezzlement to the deed. The other eleven looked on with incredulity, in shock and anger that they would have to share the honor of being chosen by Jesus with this dirty man—and the now confirmed scorn of the entire Jewish nation.

Once he admitted his heinous sins, all Matthew's friends disappeared, so it was no surprise when he blurted out what he did when confronted by Jesus. To other Jews, Matthew's participation and subsequent corruption by the greed in the Roman system was symptomatic of a fallen people integrated with their pagan occupiers. The men were hard on him, and it angered them even more that Jesus spoke of anger in their hearts being the same as murder. It shocked them that he took this stance rather than chastising Matthew for his gross negligence of loyalty to the Jewish people.

Even in repentance and forgiveness, and being chosen as one of the twelve, the fishermen in particular would not forget what they had forgiven. Matthew found himself in a lower social class among the twelve; he often sat next to the young Iscariot boy, as Judas was referred to from time to time. Once a pecking order was established, it was interesting to note that

Jesus did not mind some partition between the men. Though he never qualified it, he certainly did not condemn it. This was a mystery to Matthew as well as the others. Why would he not stand up for Matthew? Did he expect him to fight? Indeed, at times they would argue and debate until close to dawn. Jesus allowed their humanity; this was most interesting to Judas.

As the men learned of Jesus' ways, they also learned how to stretch their faith. Jesus paired them up and sent them out to preach. This was a major turning point for young Judas. He was paired with Thomas, and Judas quickly discovered while walking with his newfound friend that he possessed the greater leadership attributes.

As they ventured forth, the instructions given them were simple, but they also produced ambiguity that required decision-making. Thomas was wont to pray for guidance, while Judas was ready to walk on and get on with it. In truth, Judas wanted to see if he really had the faith needed to complete the task—even if it displayed itself in simply opening his mouth.

> He was paired with Thomas, and Judas quickly discovered while walking with his newfound friend that he possessed the greater leadership attributes.

As the months wore on, Jesus finally gave the twelve some authority. It was a measured amount, to be sure, but authority nonetheless. They were to travel—and preach and heal and drive out demons as they went. The disciples had been itching for this moment. At the same time, they were in awe of their instructions and in awe that they might have what it took to perform some of the very same miracles as Jesus. The wrestling match had begun. Now the learning was participatory: they had to put themselves to the test. Observation time was over. To a man, none of them believed they could do such miracles.

As with most men, thoughts of divinity were quickly arrested by thoughts about self. It was a quiet battle, but one they all faced: how would Jesus' power flow through them, and how would they act in response? Would the power somehow be conditioned upon how empty they were of personal ambition, or did it matter? It was all new, and far beyond the bounds of typical instruction from a rabbi.

So young Judas and Thomas carried on. Thomas's timidity annoyed Judas to no end. "Can't we just stop and pray? We need to pray, young Judas." He would have to practically beg Judas to slow down, to stop and not be so *youthful* about it all. "Fine, have it your way." Prayer was almost absurd to Judas at this point; they were walking with Jesus, for mercy's sake, and he had already delegated authority over spirits, so what was there to pray about? Judas would acquiesce and let Thomas do the praying on his own. He wanted to get on with the experiment, he wanted to heal, and if he were honest with himself, he still needed confirmation that he was indeed among the chosen.

The first order of business for the two men was to secure lodging. Thomas and Judas split up, but not without much discussion; Thomas wanted to obey Jesus and stay as a team. Judas had to explain that they were a team; they were just separating for a task. Judas began to wonder if Thomas were not touched in some way mentally. Simply getting Thomas motivated always seemed a challenge for Judas. *Some chosen one,* Judas would think.

But it was Thomas who would secure their place to stay. Judas knocked on several doors, but to no avail. Thomas managed to find housing at his first knock. They stayed with a widow for three nights as they advanced toward Bethany.

It was there they witnessed their first miracle of their own delivery.

She was a sick young girl. They had mentioned their task and calling, and the widow made certain they knew of the young girl's plight. Without delay, they made their way there.

The girl had been bedridden for several months and had taken nothing but occasional corned bread and water. The entire house reeked of urine, and the flies were horrendous. Judas could not wait to leave. They were ushered into the back, where the girl was laying on a cushion of sorts in a corner. She was on the ground, and the cushion was actually matting made of sacks, not unlike the harvest cloths and sacks Judas was accustomed to using.

The others in the house, desperate enough to let these two strangers in, huddled around them. To them, this was a perfunctory pre-burial ritual, another step farther down the path of death for the girl. Just one more holy man and his charges doing their duty for the sick. One woman, presumably the girl's mother, stood motionless, almost without emotion, at her side. She was the sad display of a sad people—desperate and without hope. Judas and Thomas both felt their pain. It was unlike anything they had witnessed.

The small group's sadness permeated the hearts of Judas and Thomas. So did a sudden rush of pressure to perform. Would it work? Were they strong enough to be proper conduits for Jesus? Would he really allow them to? Did they truly have faith?

As they knelt, the girl lay awake, but her eyes were heavy, fixed with shock, and she did not move. They explained that they were sent to heal and would do so in the name of Jesus without expecting anything in return. Judas went first, and as he began to pray, a fly landed on the girl's lower lip. He waved it away and continued. Once he finished, Thomas also prayed over her. They looked at each other, placed her hands in theirs, and said the word: "Rise."

She blinked twice, then smiled. Then she sat up. The sad little group stirred suddenly, one man grabbing at the two apostles, as if they were hurting her. It was as if they wanted her to lie back down. Almost as if they wanted her to stay sick. She turned to the woman—indeed, it was her mother—and cried tears of joy, hugging her all the while. Everyone gathered around, and Thomas and Judas backed away. The entire house was amazed and praised God, shaking the men's hands and hugging them. Though they were begged to stay, eat, and celebrate, they left shortly afterward, remembering the example of their rabbi.

It was disconnecting to heal someone. Their hands felt nothing. Their bodies did nothing. They spoke, and the person would walk or get up or feel better. Doubts raced through their minds. They were anticipating a warm feeling or a tremor inside—*something* to indicate there was a power greater than themselves at work. But nothing like that came. *Maybe Jesus has gone before us and set all this up;* Judas had this fleeting thought, derived from his aunt's seed, still in his mind. But no. There was no way Jesus could do all this for all six groups of men. It had to be real.

There was much excitement when the men returned. Similar stories were shared, and Jesus was smiling. Judas had time to share, and though there was still a hint of condescension, it was clear that the healing and preaching had brought joy to the men, but more importantly, humility. They had all lost a few years of humanity but also gained the perspective

There was much excitement when the men returned. Similar stories were shared, and Jesus was smiling. of faith that was something like a child at a festival. Jesus calmed them, raising his hands to ease the discussion, telling them to rejoice not in all that they had seen and done, but that they were accepted by God in Heaven. But for the most part, these were wasted words. They were far too excited at what they had done. They were human.

Jesus had been preaching for some time and had gained a respectful reputation, and the men made a stop at James and John's parents' lower city dwelling. They were welcomed into the home and stayed there several nights. For the brothers, it was home, so they found an additional energy they had lacked in other spots. Judas was reminded of the serenity of his mother's care, and imagined these men had benefited from the same. Judas suddenly found himself missing home.

On their final night there, James and John's mother was anxious, and Jesus smiled to her and said she would find comfort in her sons' lives. No one was sure what that meant, but she could not help herself in replying, and practically blurted out that she would have her sons be on Jesus' right and left when the time came. The look of smugness on their faces was enough to incite a riot, save for Jesus putting her in her place, saying that the Father would place things as He saw fit in Heaven. Such a strange conversation, and arrogance—both on the part of the woman and Jesus, Judas thought. Like he could command such things, or even comment on them to begin with.

This desire and request from James and John's mother was seen as more of a proclamation to the others, since they had spent time watching the brewing relationships between

Jesus, Peter, and the two brothers. This conversation was the straw that broke the camel's back. There was a sharp dispute among the men that lasted well into the night. Though Jesus had settled the immediate request, there was still a ranking in Heaven—at least, a perceived one—that would continue to bother some of the men, and for quite some time.

As the months passed, Judas noticed a pattern. In fact, all of them did. Three of the twelve were receiving a bit more teaching and training and attention than the rest. "If you chose twelve, must you also choose between them even more?" Judas wondered aloud, yet under his breath. It made no sense to them. Jesus kept the same smile, the same teaching for all, but when Cephas (or Simon, as he was called) spoke up, Jesus taught him, spoke to him. The others, it seemed, were taught **He was selective. The other disciples saw this too, and it was not fair or acceptable, Judas thought.** as a collective, in generalized conversation. Other times, when the others would speak up, it seemed that Jesus rarely chose to reply directly or teach. He was selective. The other disciples saw this too, and it was not fair or acceptable, Judas thought.

Judas was in charge of the money, though. They had cast lots early on, and the lot fell to the young man. It was almost a comedic routine, these men casting lots in the presence of Jesus, whom some had referred to as the Messiah from the very beginning. It was a simple exercise, but in the presence of divinity it was strange, like paddling a boat with their hands while the oars were within reach. The men shifted their glances from the stones to Jesus and back, several times, as if seeking his approval of the casting exercise. They were as nervous about all this as the first time they grabbed the rudder of a boat.

Casting lots was important to them, and in a way it spoke of former times and a long-ago hero, Gideon, so there seemed to be some divinity in it. Judas was pleased for this reason: Jesus' silence in speaking to Judas was brutal for a young man to endure, but when the lot was cast his way, it was at least a tacit approval of his having been chosen. At least in this he was important; he *had been* chosen.

All of this mattered materially because they needed coins as they traveled, and their funds needed to be secure.

And they traveled a great deal. They walked all over Israel. Some places were pleasant to visit; others would flatly reject them. It was nice to have some money when they found themselves in need. Judas surmised as they went that he could use the "training" he had received from the priests, and even do so while under the watchful eye of a now disciplined and principled Matthew.

And then something else happened. Judas discovered a way to pay himself. Every once in a while, Judas would take a coin or two along the way. Money was a burden, he had to carry it, and this was Judas's way of taking a certain license with the responsibility he had been given. Peter, James, and John received extra time, so Judas counted it as reasonable. Jesus never corrected him, so he continued on.

It seemed to make sense now: his running into Hillel and learning the customs of the priests. It fit that Judas would be in charge of the money.

THE TWELVE

There was great difficulty in following a man who didn't appear to sin. There was even difficulty in walking amid other accomplished men, especially when Judas was several years younger than them. For a young man who wanted to be significant, these things proved to be quite a gauntlet, and they were Judas's lot. On the one hand, he was grateful to be one of the men being trained in whatever it was they would end up doing. On the other, he was a boy among men, and though it was unnecessary, he believed he needed to make his mark.

For the first several weeks, it seemed Judas's main contribution to the meetings of the men was . . . silence. In a few instances, he had wanted to speak up, and when Jesus was speaking of growth in trees, root systems, and fruit, he saw his chance. Judas had become knowledgeable in these areas, of course, and his eagerness got the best of him. Initially, he nodded in agreement as Jesus spoke about the fruit of a tree, how it needed to bear good fruit. Judas would interject details like caring for a tree to produce its fruit, the importance of caring for the bark, pruning the branches—many of the things he had learned on the farm. Once he had emptied himself of his life's knowledge—the grove, and farming in the grove—he felt stupid and inadequate all over again.

There were plenty of sneers to go around, and more than a few headshakes. The body language after he spoke communicated exactly what Judas was thinking: *Who am I to instruct these men?* Jesus smiled and concurred with his young disciple, and then there were smiles from others. Judas had done well in speaking up, and after the talk broke up, James put a hand on his shoulder and whispered some wise words. "Quit while you're ahead, young man."

The problem Judas faced, as did all the men, was trying to discern if Jesus was actually speaking about trees, or if he meant something altogether different. It was easy to be wrong or misguided when conversing with Jesus. So Judas would learn to stay silent. Silence was safe.

> It was easy to be wrong or misguided when conversing with Jesus. So Judas would learn to stay silent. Silence was safe.

"You never learn anything while speaking," his father would say. Judas was at least wise enough to remember that.

Then one day it happened. Jesus had just finished giving Peter a lesson in humility. What it pertained to was irrelevant to Judas. When Peter returned to the others, he was distraught and openly wrestling with whatever it was Jesus had said. Judas found himself staring at this man, easily a decade older than him, but Judas noted he was acting like one of his younger siblings. Peter took note, and that was the beginning of the end of their relationship.

"What are you looking at?" Peter stabbed.

"Uh, nothing. I . . . I was just . . . "

"You were just what? Sitting there with your mouth shut again? You're part of this too, you know. You can't just get a pass on everything. You sit there all smug like you're an idiot, but I know you're smarter than that. You think you're just going to learn things and move on without hearing from him, don't you? You're too much of a coward to speak up."

"No, I don't—"

"Well, you're right about that. You'll get your turn. Too bad you're too scared to open your mouth and be wrong once or twice—it might just make you smarter, you know." Peter paused, self-correcting along the way. He knew he was in the wrong. Instead of Matthew or Thomas, Judas was the target of his anger this time. He sighed. Perhaps Jesus' tutelage was making a difference.

"Sorry, kid. Maybe you're better off clamming up. Save you the heartache." He sneered. "Just keep sitting there and doing as you're told."

So Judas obeyed. But he never forgot. All this time he'd been following, not saying much of anything—save once. And all this time, in doing nothing, he had gained for himself a reputation. And now he knew what Peter thought of him, deep down. He wondered if the other men thought that . . . that he was just a kid. Whether they thought it or not, they definitely did not approve of the manner in which Judas was addressed by Peter, but he was a leader among them. Indeed, he was the preeminent one, marked by Jesus when Peter proclaimed Jesus as the Christ.

Other times, Judas was straight-out insulted by the others. It was not as a deliberate measure, like the one delivered by Peter, but he felt habitually ostracized. This is what really got under Judas's skin. The men would talk, sometimes deep into the night, concerning kingdom matters, with Jesus resting or in prayer, or even with Jesus himself. When the talk would shift toward Judas, however, it was the afterthought of a question, an assumption that the young one had little or nothing to add. Other times, they would simply change the subject and invite Judas into the conversation once the mental work slowed. These men would be meting out important opinions and working on their plan of attack for the kingdom of God in this world—all without input or inclusion of one of the men whom Jesus had expressly chosen. Judas's silence cost him any true position he had sought. His significance, he told himself, would have to lie elsewhere.

> Judas's silence cost him any true position he had sought. His significance, he told himself, would have to lie elsewhere.

He would be coddled, taken to the side a few times, and given consoling words by some of the men. Matthew, for one, knew what oppression was like, and he knew what it was to be its subject. At least he was kind enough to care about him, Judas thought. Some of the men simply told him to buck up, that hard knocks were a way of life regardless of who they were following. But Matthew continued to talk to Judas, instructing him in trusting God and in employing the talents he had been given.

"Pay him no mind," he would say of Peter. "Many men are insecure, and he is no exception." Judas did not see weakness or insecurity when he saw Peter. Matthew may have been right, but in the eyes of Judas, Peter was a strong man—able, forceful. He envied Peter. In fact, he envied all of them, not merely due to their age and accomplishments, but for their lack of timidity, their drive, their confidence.

Matthew would encourage him to be small, to take his place in the back, to be grateful. And one more thing: to be mindful of the great examples of men of little or no renown who had ascended to greatness. Judas would begin to get angry. He knew Matthew was going to speak of King David, and of course Matthew did. Judas received a small sermon from Matthew about the legendary king of centuries past, and was thus instructed to imitate David's life. "Trusting God," he explained, "was both the beginning and ending of our great king's legacy. It is a quality all of us should imitate."

It was easier to speak these stories, Judas thought. No one had to walk in his shoes.

The months wore on. Judas would hang tough. The discipline of a now distant farm life had not been lost on him.

HARDENED

The more they traveled, the more Jesus taught, and the tougher things became. There used to be crowds all the time. Now there were crowds until Jesus talked and challenged them. The teachings were becoming more pointed, if possible, and even though he had picked the twelve, as they were called, it seemed as if he was weeding out as many as he was inspiring. It was strange, and the disciples around Jesus would often look at him a second or third time when he laid out his challenges.

Every time there was a conversation, a request, or a beggar, the guys would play small games in their minds, trying to figure out how Jesus would handle it. Would he rebuke them, would he challenge them, would he simply smile and hug and love? It was a tough task. Their discipline and training, most times, seemed to lie in simple observation.

On one such occasion, a rich merchant, pious and learned, approached Jesus. He had several friends with him, and these were eager to back their leader's words. The disciples found it difficult to restrain themselves from coming close to the man, introducing themselves, and inviting him to join them. He was impressive, young, vibrant. He also seemed blameless. The men's minds raced ahead, wondering if they would be adding a thirteenth member to their little band. As Judas well knew, it didn't hurt to have someone in the know accompanying them, someone in a moneyed position, someone who could give them leverage. Thoughts from his days with Hillel filled Judas's mind.

Jesus did exactly what the men *didn't* want. He looked directly at the young man, put his hand on his shoulder, like father to a son, and said, "Go and sell everything you have, and give it to the poor you see here before you. Then, your treasure will be in Heaven, and you may follow me." The wind left everyone's sails after that. It only seemed fair to the rest of the men, once they thought it through. But the merchant turned and left. After a few steps, he looked back—somewhat like a child who wants his father to change his mind when told he can't play in the field. Once he saw nothing favorable, he turned back with his group, sulking on his way. There would be no thirteenth man added—at least, not with this one.

It was like that now, as the ministry continued on. Many people were leaving. The challenges were stiff and controversial. Their community associations increasingly became with the untouchables, the downtrodden, with those who had no one else to turn to, no other hope. This made things difficult, but the men also found it somewhat nice not to have so many people constantly crowding around.

Jesus was always teaching, and always correcting, but he never let loose the anger that everyone knew was in him. He was perfectly patient in every area, in every conversation—except for once. They had approached the temple courts and Jesus was bantering back and forth with the disciples. Peter had been boasting, as was his pattern, about the number of fish he could catch. The tales were tiresome to many of them, but Judas loved to hear them. Judas, of course, had no tales to tell—no storms, no ripped sails, no huge hauls of fish. Just olives. Lots and lots of olives. Jesus was complimentary of Peter, yet also managed to look at him sideways when Peter was bluffing. Jesus would simply say, slowly, "Is that so, Peter?" And everyone would laugh, knowing Peter had been caught. A fisherman's tales were tough around Jesus.

But this day, as they walked into the courts, Jesus just stopped. No more smiling, no more joking. Jesus walked over to the side, to a vendor selling leather cordage for tents. He motioned to Judas. "Judas, give this man whatever he asks for a price on these strips, the ones I'm going to take. They are special to me."

Judas answered, "But, Lord, these are shorter than the ones up the street, and they're overpriced. We can walk back and get more for less. Our pouch is thin as it is."

"I know, Judas. I know. Please do as I ask. These will be fine."

Judas obeyed. His default was to obey. It didn't come naturally, but the years spent serving his father had conditioned his mind almost as strongly as they had conditioned his body. He could always bring the matter up later, he thought. Jesus never bought anything—at least, not that Judas could think of—so he was interested to see what Jesus was doing.

Jesus sat down and, without speaking to anyone, began to string several strips of the leather together. Every few seconds, he would look up, not at the disciples, but at the people walking, buying, selling, joking, and laughing their way through the maze of markets in the temple court. It seemed a pleasant scene to Judas. Then Jesus would shake his head and go back to methodically wrapping and weaving the strips together.

Up until now, Jesus' hands were spent in prayer, in gesturing to the crowds, helping people rise, caressing faces, and holding children. Jesus' hands were strong, though, and Judas remembered Jesus had spent his early years as a carpenter. It made Judas think of his father's powerful hands. He blinked, and it was back to the task at hand. Once Jesus had four or five cords in a lengthy rope with both ends loose, about two or three feet in length, he wrapped a sixth strip around the base of the others on one end, tied off the end, and tucked it neatly into the base.

He'd made a whip.

Jesus rose from his place, walked deliberately into the crowd, and began swinging the woven cords wildly at all the livestock and their handlers in the court. At first, the men started to follow, but once he began swinging, they all dropped back. In fact, as Jesus cleared out every area in which he walked, they found themselves apologetically plodding along behind him in the wake of this terror. He seemed to scold practically everyone present.

"How dare you? What has happened to you? This is my

Father's house! His sanctuary! And you have turned it into a market! . . . Shame is upon you for this! . . . Get out! All of you—now!" Dust rose quickly as the merchants and people scattered. It was all happening so fast. Many priests came running out of the temple itself, at first curious and then determined, like a parent scolding his children for playing too loudly. When they saw what was happening, they stopped and stared in disbelief. He had, in only a few minutes, scared everyone, angered most people in the crowds, and wrecked an entire area. Dust and dirt were all over every merchant's table. Chickens, doves, calves, and sheep were everywhere. Between scrambling to retrieve their animals, people were cursing Jesus, yelling at him to clean things up, clamoring at him and the twelve. John had to restrain a man who just missed punching Jesus while the man was scrambling to retrieve his wares.

The rest of the disciples stood there in shock. They scarcely even looked at each other. Then Jesus walked up to the table of the moneychangers. The disciples' eyes widened. Would he whip them as well? Jesus clamped firmly onto the table with his free hand, paused for a second, and then threw the table, end over end, across the messy courtyard. Money went everywhere. Then he dropped the whip, turned, and walked back up the steps, right past the teachers and priests. They parted like the Red Sea, and Jesus and the disciples walked directly through to the temple, leaving a chaotic, dust-filled wake.

That night, after prayers, not much talking was done—not even by Peter. Jesus was a complete man, and he was also much larger than that. An ordinary man would have been arrested, but Jesus was showing his twelve that the rules of men were no match for true conviction. All of the men realized something that day: Jesus was serious. Judas and the others were overwhelmed yet again.

Jesus issued stiff challenges to the disciples at times, even going so far as to rebuke them when they stepped badly out of line. It reminded Judas of the scolding he would receive when he stepped on olives, ruined branches, or fought with his siblings. Only, with Jesus, the admonitions were more consistent. At one point, he looked up to Heaven and said, through gritted teeth, "How long must I tolerate you?" It was a steady stream of correction and learning during the day, but more a tone of encouragement to the men at night, when the crowds died down.

On the other hand, it was amazing how commonplace it became to see miracles. It was not as if the men had become hardened to it all, or become expectant. For the life of them, not one could predict when Jesus would display his power. When Jesus would stop, speak, or touch anyone, however, no matter how often they saw something unbelievable happen, they would stop and watch.

There was eagerness among the twelve, and for quite a while they would try to anticipate how Jesus would heal or what he would command. It was not impossible, only improbable, and definitely luck, if one of them got it right. On the one hand they were receiving training, instruction unlike anything the world had ever seen or would ever see again. On the other hand, they felt a great deal like children with a parent: under protection, secure, safe. But even now, the miracles were finished with a warning or instruction. Often, it

> Jesus was showing his twelve that the rules of men were no match for true conviction. All of the men realized something that day: Jesus was serious.

didn't seem much fun anymore. Maybe he was getting sick of it, Judas would think. Maybe he was just tired.

Then there was a pivotal day, a sermon from Jesus that really solidified it for the men, that cut to the heart of what everyone was thinking. What was typical, even in a moment of revelation, was that clarification from Jesus often created more questions. This day would be no different. All along there seemed to be two lines of thought running side by side alongside Jesus, and on this day, Jesus would veer right into the existing priesthood, into the Old Covenant, and introduce a new one.

They were in the northern town of Capernaum, and they were doing what, by now, was so unusual to the masses and yet routine to them: preaching, healing, and the like. They had received permission to speak in the local synagogue, even with—or perhaps because of—Jesus' actions in recent weeks. The love, respect, and adoration Jesus had gained was being weighed by those who had received it even while they were also seeking to understand a sort of new morality. It began to dawn on the disciples that this may be the last time they would have permission to enter a holy place. If the whipping of people and animals didn't do it, this day certainly would.

It began to dawn on the disciples that this may be the last time they would have permission to enter a holy place.

Jesus began, as usual, with Scripture, but quickly began to describe a new way of thinking, a new way of living. It became a no-turning-back point for the twelve. He started with a statement about being the bread of life, and before they knew it (they would often catch themselves half-listening and half-watching the various reactions), Jesus had said that unless people "eat my flesh" and "drink my blood" they were dead. Now all eyes were strictly fastened on him—even the twelve. What had Jesus just said? They exchanged nervous looks. No matter. There was much grumbling among the people, and talk quickly ensued that this madman had to be stopped.

Suddenly, everything became extremely uncomfortable; things were teetering toward violence. There was not a safe place to be had, in any conversation, and the large crowd that had gathered was now quickly dwindling. Jesus had just fed thousands of people, and now there were less than seventy standing around him. Indeed, many of them stayed merely because they were curious what crazy thing would come from this man next. It was a tough thing to reconcile. On the one hand, Jesus had performed an unthinkable miracle: the actual multiplication of food. On the other, he was now implying that his body was going to be food, and that those who didn't believe this would be dead—at least spiritually dead.

As people left the synagogue, there was a wild gleam in Jesus' eye. He turned to the twelve, looking intense and yet somehow calm, if that were possible, and said, "Are you leaving too?" It was a moment of decision Judas would never forget. He felt it was not fair. He felt forced to make a split-second decision. The twelve were not afforded the time to ask Jesus about this; they did not have the mental space to adjust to the words, to make sense of them, to decipher the code Jesus had so often used. He was asking if they really, *truly* believed him or not. On the inside, Judas was angry: how could he confront them in front of everyone? Didn't he care what they thought? How they felt? How could they possibly make a decision like

He was asking if they really, *truly* believed him or not.

this after what he had just said? Judas needed an explanation.

Naturally, Peter spoke up first. He said they would stay, would remain, because only Jesus had the answers. Peter was such a social and loyal man.

It was so easy for Peter to diffuse a dangerous situation, one that had the potential to scatter them all to the hills until they could figure out what they truly thought.

Jesus jumped on Peter's proclamation. Judas felt it was smug: "Have I not chosen you twelve? But one of you is the devil!" Everyone glanced at Matthew and then glanced down. No one knew what he meant, and no one asked. In truth, they did not want to know, at least not now. It would have been crushing to any of them had they known that Jesus considered them a devil.

In truth, Judas felt like the devil half the time, as did the others, whenever they sinned. In the presence of perfection, there is constant exposure, constant scrutiny, and constant correction—even when one does not speak. The presence of God among them was the most humbling thing any of them would experience, and Judas loved this aspect of things, at those times that he *felt* the presence of God. Like the others, though, he would despise it at times as well. Being with Jesus was as safe as a mother's song, and yet as intimidating as a father's hand. Being in this group was not for the faint of heart, or for the man lacking wisdom. It was *real*. In time, all of this proved to be too much of a good thing for Judas, and that would be the difference.

There was talk early in his ministry that the people would

make Jesus king, but he always seemed to somehow elude the most intense spotlight. Despite the desire of the crowds for him, he did not take praise, but gave it to God. But the people kept following *him*, not God. Now he was claiming that life was found in and through him and through his flesh and blood. *How could that be?* If you give praise to God, Judas thought, how can you claim that people need to follow you? It made no sense—along with about half of what Judas had swimming around in his head.

He was not alone in some of these thoughts; the men would often discuss these matters after Jesus left them alone. The problem for Judas, of course, was that many of these discussions excluded him. It was natural, and he had been put in his place more than once, usually by one of the more outspoken among them, and even once by Matthew. He truly had become the least among the twelve, and this made intimate discussions almost impossible. Judas was left to his own devices many times, simply listening to glean what he could without getting his questions and doubts addressed by the men.

One issue that no one could resolve, which actually served to bring Judas a bit closer to the rest, was Jesus' focus on the three men he had chosen among the twelve. It was as if Peter, James, and John would be the leaders, though Jesus never directly set them over the others. They simply received more attention. The rest of them were left to find their own voices of leadership. It made for grumbling more often than not, and Judas was no exception. Each man still struggled with envy for spots in leadership, as well as the desire to be in Jesus' inner circle. Judas was used to being left out, having been passed over by every rabbi and opportunity earlier in life. The lesser attention received from Jesus too often seemed like outright rejection. And it hurt. Did Jesus love him—the nine of them?—less? Did he love the other three more? It was difficult for a young man to swallow.

He could become a leader in his own right, Judas told himself. He would have no choice. The men would grumble, and Judas would remain silent. Inside, however, Judas was becoming hurt, even enraged. *Why not me?* Judas felt ignored, and now an outcast, all over again. His quest for significance seemed to continue to dwindle. And then, this thought would go through his mind: He was chosen *last*, after all.

Judas soon found himself "taxing" Jesus' choices. He would take coins more frequently, especially and particularly when Jesus would pass him over—even if the slight were imaginary. If it was going to be James, John, and Peter in the end, at least Judas could go back to the farm with some money. It kept Judas sane, as he was beginning to be eaten up by his own mind. Jesus never scolded him, never even spoke to him of his theft, though he must have known. He seemed to know everything. Judas was as convinced as any of them that Jesus was, at the very least, a prophet ordained by God himself, if not the Messiah. That made stealing all the more significant to Judas—his lack of discipline by the all-knowing Jesus was all the proof he needed that Jesus did not deeply love him or truly care about him. Perhaps Jesus didn't have any plans for him other than letting him follow along and carry money.

Their relationship had always seemed to be a conversation of the eyes. Judas often looked there, not to try to make a connection, but to see if Jesus was a real man behind those eyes. Was he just some crazed teacher of the law, making his pronouncements, seeking fame? Of course not. That was well established by now. But could Jesus really discern between right and wrong? It had become obvious when a man would speak some ill that he was wrong, and not just to Jesus but to everyone in the group. But could he see sin in the eyes of a man even if that man had not spoken? It was this curiosity that stuck with Judas.

Judas never forgot the first time he took money. It was legitimate enough, as he had bought bread for the little band of vagabonds as they ventured just outside Jerusalem. There was a crowd as usual, and as Jesus led them out, he instructed Judas to serve his brothers by making the purchase. Judas felt some honor at being given the responsibility, but there was also a perceived slight in it. He was being relegated to errand boy, and this bothered him. It was one thing being passed by because of age or maturity; in fact, by the nature of having twelve of them, some of the others experienced this as well. But even in his father's grove he had authority, some semblance of respect, and responsibility that rivaled any adult who would be in their employ. Was he merely chosen to be a servant? These men were entrusted with great things, and Judas was merely serving.

There was change remaining from the purchase of bread, and Judas bought himself a snack of apricots and pocketed the rest. Upon return to the camp, there was still considerable talk and mild commotion over the events arising from the latest crowd—events that Judas had missed. Jesus thanked Judas for purchasing the bread, as did the others, and smiled mildly. It may have been love, it may have been disappointment; Judas wasn't sure. One thing was sure: it wasn't correction, so Judas took it as permission.

As time went on, the maturation of Peter became evident.

He always was speaking, it seemed, and often put his foot in his mouth. But one occasion, not unlike the discussion about eating his flesh, sealed the men's hearts to Jesus—and sealed Peter as their leader.

One afternoon, Jesus struck up a conversation with the men. It was atypical, as he was normally peppered by their questions, dogged by their pained insights, their constant curiosities. But this day Jesus asked some questions. They were making their way through the tent cities on the outskirts of Caesarea Philippi, and Jesus was describing to them the many types of people—their hearts, thoughts, triumphs, defeats, and dreams. They moved to a private area, and Jesus knelt with them in prayer. They did not know what to make of this change in course but, naturally, they knelt beside him.

Once he finished his prayer, he turned.

"Who do the people say the Son of Man is?"

Silence. Then Andrew, who was a coward of a man in Judas's eyes, chimed in with what they had all heard from time to time. "Some say John the Baptist, some say Elijah, Jeremiah, or one of the other prophets." It was Andrew's typical response: a release from responsibility of independent thought, the act of merely restating what they had all heard before.

"What about *you*? Who do *you* say I am?"

Again, silence. Then Peter: "You are the Christ, the son of the living God."

What happened next was one of those whirlwind moments in which Jesus explained something, proclaimed something, and sang something at the same time. It was what the men referred to as a "prophetous" time.

"Blessed are you, Simon son of Jonah—God has revealed this to you, not men. From now on you will be called Peter, and on this rock I will build my distinct following, and the gates of Hell will not stand to it. From now on it is understood that you will have the keys to the Kingdom of Heaven—what you bind for there will stand, and what you release will wither."

The men went from a somewhat normal conversation with their master to confusion and astonishment. Other men had seen and experienced exactly what Simon—now called Peter—had seen and experienced. But to Peter was given great responsibility and authority. The men felt and thought the response, but Peter had *spoken* it. He did not have cowardice when he was with his master, and it showed. The others were lacking that confidence, and they withered at such a question. For Peter it was easy, and his pronouncement would catapult him firmly into the leadership position among these leaders. Even James and John tapered their jealousy a bit, knowing that they were being groomed as well, but that it was on Peter that divinity had truly shined. Peter would be withered later by other, different questions.

> The men felt and thought the response, but Peter had *spoken* it.

Judas and Thomas were still together, having been sent out once again as a pair. The men surmised that if the Lord saw fit to pair them for an assignment, perhaps they should fit themselves together for much of the rest of the time. The relationship between the two had grown, and they naturally walked close in heart. They heard this latest conversation and proclamation together as well. Judas was sulking, angry. Thomas was inspired. In Judas's mind, Jesus may well have orchestrated the whole thing just to publicly declare his favorite.

The show did not stop that day. Jesus immediately sat with the men, explaining to them something that furrowed every brow. He would be handed over to the rulers and killed. It was too much for all of them to handle. There was a ruckus that night as well; everyone pledged to stand by Jesus, and yet it was as if they still did not understand. How could the most powerful man to walk the earth, who had performed so many miracles, and given them such confidence . . . how could he who knew men's hearts not keep this from happening? Especially, if not particularly, because he was supposed to be the Messiah?

Judas thought Jesus had finally gone crazy. What gives, he would think, that the so-called Son of God couldn't stop attracting attention to himself? Judas knew there was a war raging in his mind. He would have so many conversations between him and Jesus he could no longer remember which ones he actually *had*, which ones he *wished* he had, and which were from his restless dreams.

One thing was certain to Judas: Jesus and he were splitting apart. When they had formal meals, which wasn't often, Judas would always sit next to him. At first, Judas took it as a huge compliment, and much to the consternation of the rest of the men, Jesus initiated at least this one placement when they dined. Judas initially felt this very special, but as he evolved in his knowledge and thinking, Judas began to think the placement was out of pity, or maybe to use him as an example to others that they should serve and cater to the younger ones among them. Perhaps, even, it was a way to love the thief by keeping him close.

All of this began to bother Judas, almost indescribably so.

Now sitting next to him became fairly uncomfortable. He was slow to laugh with the men, but he would learn to keep up a smile, keep up the façade. His eagerness to sit at Jesus' side was haunting him. The other men would joke continually, and many times Judas's lack of laughter spoke of his youth and inexperience. What no one else knew was that, inside, a storm of jealousy, hatred, and envy had been brewing.

ON ANGER

"Now, don't be angry after you've been afraid—
that's the worst kind of cowardice."
—Rudyard Kipling[3]

Anger is comfort for the tortured soul. If we ignore the fuel source, we can burn that anger through the atmosphere around us as long as we want. It changes us. We suddenly find some weird, wicked version of ourselves, ready to do whatever is past the line we've drawn in the sands of our conscience.

When someone is treated unjustly, there are two paths that emerge: *sorrow* at being treated in such a way; and *stress* arising from the discrepancy between what should have happened and what actually took place. The response of sorrow at being wronged often leads to internal anger and blossoms into guilt, depression, and/or shame—i.e., "I deserved this." The stress response is what results in external anger. The stress arises from the attempt to reconcile what the victim believes he or she should have experienced with the actual events. ("You were supposed to save money but you wasted it on that?" "You are supposed to listen to me, but you're just talking over me." And so on.) Anger is the *expression* of stress when a person—even ones' self—mishandles a real or perceived injustice. In more extreme cases, both the sorrow and stress response reside and anger ensues.

Anger is frequently staved off by the self-justification that arises from being wronged. It is tempered, covered, filtered away by excuses and reasoning until it can no longer contain itself. Anger is hurt realized and expressed: a person's vain attempt to self-medicate a sort of peace with or without accompanying revenge. Many times we open our mouths in anger, only to speak words we don't mean or to express opinions and convictions that point to another larger, hidden issue within ourselves.

> Anger is the *expression* of stress when a person— even one's self— mishandles a real or perceived injustice.

Jesus' presence on earth set loose all of mankind's experiences and perceptions about himself and his Creator in a compressed time. Men and women can vacillate for days, weeks, even years concerning the question of whether to follow Jesus. In first-century Palestine that decision was brought upon men and women in force—and daily, with every interaction, miracle, speech, and correction given by Jesus. At every turn, people were astounded, convicted, confused, and confronted by their spiritual reality. How this translated into real life for the apostles was to force them to come to grips with disturbing information about their lives, their families, their society, and the Man in front of them—all in real time. This would be a tall mountain for anyone to climb—especially young Judas. He entered town and, with no warning, went from a curious but determined teen to becoming part of the first and only group to physically walk the earth with the King of the Jews. Judas had to come to grips with his ever-burgeoning desire to be significant in the midst of the most significant of men, all while being the presumed least of the chosen twelve. The incidents with the twelve—Peter's derision toward Judas, Judas's strained interactions with Matthew—along with Jesus' perceived indifference, and Judas's internal angst—all had to be reconciled with Jesus' teachings of how to live in a new covenant. Judas's fear and insecurities became fertile ground for unrest and stress to grow into anger.

Every area in which Judas would try and pull ahead would be met with scorn, rebuke, or simply dulled by others' more forceful attempts to rise in leadership. Someone who, in comparison to the rest of the twelve, was so seemingly insignificant, would arguably become the most important apostle in a theological sense. How might this be true? Without the catalyst of a broken-down Judas, we do not have the necessary betrayer to send Jesus to the cross. His anger would fuel his ambition, and his voice became the oppressor of truth. His agreements with hardhearted men would propel him to a sad place of extreme significance. The irony, of course, is his desire for significance would spell his demise—a sudden flirtation with fame exposed him and his plans, and his anger sealed his fate.

> Someone who, in comparison to the rest of the twelve, was so seemingly insignificant, would arguably become the most important apostle in a theological sense.

Jim

I've had the privilege of sharing life with Jim over the last decade. Jim's upbringing could best be summarized in the following collection of words: "When it was around 5 p.m., my siblings and I would look around the house and hide the heavy things because Dad would be home soon." Most of us cannot relate to an upbringing where one minute finds us sitting at the table doing homework and the next we are nursing a bloody lip from a dad who decided we needed punched in the face. A child's reaction toward an unjust action from a parent is humbling to all of us. Rather than fight back, they immediately justify the parent's action, cowering in shame and fear. *There must have been some reason for this.* It is classic co-dependency, and with justifiable reason! Mom and Dad are supposed to be the protectors, providers—and they love us, right? *If I got hit,* the child thinks, *it's because I did something to deserve it.*

Once when Jim came home from school, his father's girlfriend was in the house with her son. Jim saw this boy on top of his younger brother, choking him toward death. Jim did what he knew: he beat the other kid down as quickly as you could imagine. When his dad got home, the girlfriend made him choose: it was Jimmy or her. So, in his anger, Jim's dad kicked him out of his house for good—at the age of fourteen. In December. In the snow. Now a homeless teenager, Jim resourcefully stole a tree from behind a K-Mart and burned it for heat. He was learning survival out of pure panic and necessity—all the while building an angry resolve that nothing would get the best of him. He would live under an overpass for a year and a half, get himself a job in construction, and impressively pull himself up in life. He slept in the construction vehicles after others left for the day. He later married and settled into a life of sales, where partying and drugs became the norm. He could hang with the best of them, fueled by his anger and equipped with his father's knack for handling massive amounts of alcohol and drugs. He was but five-foot-nine, and 135 pounds soaking wet, but he was wiry. And he had anger. He won his local Toughman contest, even sparring with some big names in the early days of MMA.

Not surprisingly, Jim continued to imitate his father's party habits—and they became his own. Eventually, Jim would run into multiple entanglements with law enforcement, culminating in extended felony prison time for one particular episode. Unknown to him, Jim had been dragging a police officer along the highway after the officer attempted to reach through his car and take the keys from the ignition at a traffic stop because of Jim's intoxication. That episode—fortunately, the officer fully recovered—brought Jim two years in state prison.

And then, adding more fuel to his fire, Jim's wife was murdered while he was incarcerated. The little hope he had in a spouse who could love him in spite of the animal inside was now dead. And Jim would be out of prison soon. What a perfect recipe for a lifetime of anger, bitterness, and a badly slanted view toward the rest of life.

The tattoo across Jim's torso says it best: "Life is Pain."

I crossed paths with Jim when he was on parole. I had the opportunity to help him with employment and sit with him in Bible study. He confided that he and his siblings managed to meet up with their father at a funeral for a relative—shocked that the man had the gall to appear anywhere with family. They duly received him by delivering a severe beating, a firm and violent retort of anger for the way in which they were brought up. The temptation for retaliation for his wrongs was too strong for Jim, and he gave in to perhaps the easiest trap: a false peace that comes from revenge. Even when Jim and I worked together, we would often joke around, as men are prone to do, and spar with each other. In the back of my mind, however, I remember thinking: This guy learned to take a punch from his *dad*. I can never hurt him physically or emotionally as bad as he already is.

The hurt Jim experienced resurfaced periodically throughout life; he was void of a true relationship with God and peace. His hurt and subsequent anger culminated in multiple crimes against himself, the public, and his family. After multiple months of work with a group of people, including myself, and many conversations sharing life and piecing together a new reality and scorecard, Jim is now able to walk a new path.

He even had another meeting with his father; sadly, the parent remains stuck in a life of self-justification. In spite of his father's shortcomings, Jim now knows that anger is not the answer; peace and patience are.

Anger and hurt can be a deadly combination, and they reveal the Judas in all of us. Despite his mistakes, Jim has turned a significant page on his legacy and is now a champion in life, consulting and speaking with people on making the most of their lives in spite of the obstacles.

The Depth of Our Character?

While our personal lives and experiences may not mirror the severity of Jim's, the wrongs we have endured can easily give rise to anger that clouds judgment. Been passed over for a promotion? Someone took credit for your work? No one acknowledging your sacrifices? Spouse still doing the same irritating things? It's easy to see life through our own lenses rather than walking in another's shoes. Or, as Jesus tells us, "Do to others what you would have them do to you." We are faced with many decisions that are couched within episodes of being wronged, and we each must choose whether to walk the dark path of anger and revenge, or pick a different path, one of acknowledgment, acceptance, and a move toward peace.

A great lesson in this regard comes from an unlikely source. Marcus Luttrell, author of *Lone Survivor*, which became a famous movie with the same title, wrote that during his Navy SEAL training, commanders would routinely harass the candidates, slowly breaking them down to weed out the weak. When away on a training run, the commanders would break into a candidate's immaculate room, trash it completely, and when the man returned from the exercise, at around 2 a.m., the commanders would immediately demand a room inspection. The candidate would fail, of course, and have to scour his room and be ready to rejoin the ranks for running at 4 a.m. The reason they did this? Simple. They wanted to know the answer to this question: can the candidate handle that kind of injustice and keep going with his head screwed on straight? When he faced the most severe test of his life, being savagely hunted by Taliban in the mountains of Afghanistan, that mental discipline likely saved Luttrell's life.

The loss of personhood for a greater cause is important in any area—working a job, raising a family, being a soldier—and most importantly taking a seat at the table with God. How are we when it comes to being tested? It is true that we all reach our boundaries, where we "snap," but can we handle injustice, or perceived injustice, without losing our cool? What well can we tap into to prevent ourselves from building into a critical, angry, and divisive person, like Judas? We should not go on living using the "pressure release" that anger and rage can, in one sense, provide. We are all called to deal with issues. Many of us have children, or work with those younger than us, with less experience, or have those who look to us for leadership. We have to learn to grow in patience and deal with the depths of anger before it takes us places we should not go.

When one of my kids gets on my "last nerve" and I get angry, is that a true measure of the depth of my character? Perhaps, but perhaps it is just a sign of what is actually happening behind the scenes in my mind—other pressures that haven't been dealt with and digested properly. The question isn't if I should be angry in certain instances. The question is whether I have enough humility to make the proper amends, clean out my conscience and heart, and do the work needed to unearth the core of my anger.

It amazes me how bent out of shape people get from so many things in our current society—perceived slights, social media arguments, simply being too tired to be patient, bad car drivers . . . the list goes on. Anger was a coping mechanism for me for years. It wasn't until I settled in and got to the roots of the matters that I properly needed to that I began to unwind the tightness around my ego and allow life to happen, even if it wasn't happening in the fashion I imagined. Life may not be fair to many of us in the sense that we have "homework" to do to clear up our minds—and some things are far deeper than others—and then we must turn and face our normal daily challenges in

> The question is whether I have enough humility to make the proper amends, clean out my conscience and heart, and do the work needed to unearth the core of my anger.

real time as well. But this is what we are called to, because the legacy of anger and its fallout is strong. We are called to peace, with ourselves and others.

It's somewhat humorous to hear so many Christians state they would be able to stand up under serious persecution when in fact we cannot even turn the other cheek on small matters! As Paul would say when it came to disagreements between believers, "Why not rather be wronged?" (1 Corinthians 6:7). We are so ready to strike out in defense of ourselves and what is "right," seeking laws for protection and legislation to save us, and yet we are called by Jesus to peace and turning the other cheek! When serious trouble or even persecution comes, it is important to understand: we will in real time do what we have practiced, not suddenly default to some "principle" we only know in words.

How about you? Are you easily angered? Do you have a well-oiled machine of justification for why it's your right to be angry? Where has that gotten you? Can you handle injustice with grace and mercy toward others, or are you set to get your way? Can you be wronged, or are you a product of a revenge-filled society? People's actions are a reflection of their attitudes; if we react harshly to them, are we any better? Is peace closer to us when trials begin, or only when it's easy?

Perhaps it's time to change our practices when processing anger and hurt. Making decisions to change our scorecard pays dividends through surrender and peace; we can only control ourselves, not others. We cannot control the stakes that were placed in the ground that gave us our initial scorecard, but we can change our goals and values toward peace.

THE PROPOSITION

They were constantly walking. If they weren't staying in Capernaum, they were walking around the city and, it seemed, all over Israel. They camped here and there, wherever they could. They would usually find a place between towns or, most definitely, before they entered a town. When they managed to skirt away from one place, they would filter away the stragglers who only wanted to follow for the show. They learned Jesus' language, though many times they still did not understand why he did what he did.

"You go proclaim the Kingdom of God," he would say at times. At others, it was "Go in peace," or sometimes a more specific challenge. Sometimes it was so personal the disciples were afraid of retaliation, and many times the admonition was unbearable for the recipient. In sending away those who might otherwise have joined them, Jesus did a service to both parties. He gave space to his disciples, but it was also an act of sending the healed on a mission. This was a simple example of how Jesus was exhausting even to the disciples. They did not know his motivation: to convict and change the would-be follower to test him, or to send him away lovingly so as to move on with the ministry? When would he galvanize an army and get Israel on the map again? Trying to figure all this out was tiresome.

Though the men grew accustomed to their constant state of alertness and servitude, they needed, and loved, the nights before they would enter a town. Because, once they ventured in, it was all about Jesus, and the crowds were unforgiving. It was a chore to deal with the crowds. But then the homes they stayed in would usually be warm places, full of vibrant fellowship and food. And Jesus' lessons were taught almost constantly, it seemed. So much wisdom was being poured out without words, and even more when Jesus spoke. It was a great respite, and though they were learning, the greatest lesson may have been the fellowship. At the same time, it was a strain to be nomads and constantly borrowing the goodwill of others.

Campsites became their home away from the homes. Some of the men were more comfortable living in others' homes. Peter had his family's home, for instance, so his was not a situation of abiding with strangers on a constant basis. Since Judas's family was on the outskirts of the populated areas, and there was little room in his home, he would rarely see his family. Every meeting for Judas was new, every home not a home. If he could have, he would have admitted that he missed his mother.

Camping had its adventures. Each man had provisions to procure. The men would have to collect through the days of plenty and then save food and flint for when the weather would not be so good. They had blankets they carried for the night chill, but not much else. It was quiet in the hills, however, and the psalms they sang rang truest as they lived out their lives. But in the end, ground is still ground; the Middle Eastern sand and clay were not soft. Eventually, they would tire and sleep would come.

Both the younger and older men among them had work ethic, but some of them had to make special

> Following in any rabbi's steps had its difficulties, but following a man who believed his food was to do God's will was a difficulty no human being could adequately prepare for.

sacrifices they were not prepared for. Following in any rabbi's steps had its difficulties, but following a man who believed his food was to do God's will was a difficulty no human being could adequately prepare for. Though all of them had worked, none of them knew how to work like this. And they exercised their minds as strenuously as they beat their bodies. Their fuel source was changing. A couple of the men markedly changed shape within a few weeks; the others merely sharpened their already chiseled frames. They had fish here and there, but manna mostly, and sometimes eggs if they were lucky. But mostly bread.

The men quickly became seasoned. Once the men and women around them could see for themselves what Jesus could do, they would get no rest. They would be hounded for more, crowded out, or sent out of a town quickly. Usually, it was the former. They were all used to it, and they were all becoming comfortable with the crowds—for the most part. Late in the day was always a challenge. Patience inevitably wore thin. It was bound to because the needs never stopped, and neither, it seemed, did Jesus. His was a constant, stellar reminder, an example they could only seek to emulate.

On one such saunter through the streets, Judas was his usual wandering-eye self. Jesus was kind enough toward him, but because he seemed to pay Judas no special attention, Judas largely began shrugging off the teachings of Jesus; he began looking at them merely as good suggestions. He was simply following in the wake of the great healer while carrying a money pouch for the crew. Some of the other men had been mostly ignored also, Judas thought. They were not included in special trips Jesus would take with Peter, James, and John. But their reaction was more mature or, at the least, less self-serving. They found it a great honor to have been chosen; that had been enough.

It was not that Judas lost interest in helping people. It was not that he was completely hard of heart. But persistent thoughts stayed with him now: How many more months or years could he keep this up? How many people did Jesus need to heal? *It's obvious to everyone who he is,* Judas thought. So why not just stop with the teasing of society and fix everything? *God walking among us?* Ha! If God were among us, why would he, at times, act so feeble, so weak? It was like a bad joke. Here's the creator of all things, and he'll take you one at a time. Get in line, wait your turn. "All the while, he will speak to us and lecture us on humility while being so grandiose," Judas mumbled.

One day as he was thinking on these matters, Judas spied, from the corner of his eye, his old friend Hillel. *Strange*, Judas thought. *Why is he half-hidden like this behind some grain barrels under the tent of this seller?* Hillel looked directly at Jesus as he walked by, then cast a glare at Judas, and motioned that they should meet at one side of the market. Judas dropped back a bit, and as the crowd moved forward, he slipped over to his old friend.

"Still following this guy around? This has become rather ridiculous, hasn't it?" Hillel pried. Despite the harsh words, Judas found it a good thing to see his friend again. It had been two years or more since Judas joined with Jesus, and his eighteen-plus years now made him a man. It seemed an eternity ago that he would tease his old friend.

"Well, you know, there is such work to be done." Judas had become compliant again, all those negative thoughts drained away by the self-sustaining instinct he had cultivated through the years—the very antithesis of his Master's actual teaching.

Hillel half-chuckled as he smirked. "Yeah, whatever you say. You know this has become a nuisance to all of us. So he can supposedly heal people, so he can make people follow him around. The bottom line is he has to be stopped or the Romans will examine us more closely. I've spoken to the Ruling Council. I told them that you understand how things work in the province. This disturbance can't continue, and we both know it."

Judas had a ready reply. "Ha! What do you think? He's just going to go away? Are you proposing to get him banished from town? Good luck with the crowds then! You can't have him arrested; he hasn't done anything wrong." Judas's voice grew quieter. "And he won't just stop. He's more constant than the sun." Though Judas's words were true, his heart was in a place that was far from defending his master; he was sick of the con-

> He had become defeated. What was once doubt and personal distance in his mind had crystallized into defiance.

stant drip of need and service. Judas looked at the ground. He had become defeated. What was once doubt and personal distance in his mind had crystallized into defiance.

"Leave all of that to the Council, Judas. They just want to bring him in for questioning. Not as part of his parading himself and his teaching, but before the Council. Anyway, they want to meet you tomorrow night to gain your insight into this situation and to set up an agreement that will help us all. Will you meet them? Tomorrow night? At the wall bordering the market after sundown."

"And if I don't, then what will you do?"

Hillel stopped walking. He turned to Judas, and it was suddenly a bit more than a question or a request. He put his hand on Judas's shoulder. "The Council is fairly certain you will be able to help us. I've told them you understand how things work—no one else who is as close to this man can help. If you love your people, you will do it."

Judas sighed. "Fine. I'll do it, Hillel." He paused. "What can it hurt anyway?"

"OK, I'll let them know." As he turned to leave, Hillel stated the obvious to young Judas: "And don't tell any of them."

"Do you think I'm a fool? I'm no idiot, you know." Judas walked off. The last thing he needed was to be lectured about whom to tell what. Hillel didn't realize who he was dealing with now. He knew the best course to take. He would meet with them, he would see what they want.

Now the talk in Judas's mind had changed—from being

upset with Jesus to grumbling about Hillel. He appreciated the friendship they shared, but suddenly he felt stretched. And a bit like a pawn.

He needed to catch up to the others before they sensed anything.

16

ON FEAR

"Courage is feeling fear, not getting rid of fear,
and taking action in the face of fear."
—Roy T. Bennett[4]

It doesn't need to win or even be dominant. It doesn't need to trump other emotions, memories, or thoughts. It just needs to *be there*—sometimes in a whisper, sometimes in a scream, sometimes something in between. It just needs to be a constant and contribute to tweaking the decision-making abilities of its host. It is the fuel and the yeast by which all other emotions grow or die. It kills love, feeds anger, blossoms embarrassment, and shoves sadness toward depression. Bridled fear, or absence thereof, equals happiness and peace. Fear of embarrassment or injustice breeds anger. It is the struggle and grappling for a foothold of security somewhere in our minds.

Fear. It is one of the first ingredients in the devil's inventory of tools.

Fear is often used as a motivator by those who seek to conquer areas of their lives. It propels people to dare and reveals
the risk-taking side of us. It helps us do things we normally
would never do, and it can stop us from doing the things we
should.

The first step out the door in the direction of where we can't
see a clear path is our introduction to fear. The unknowns of
life that surround us are not necessarily the cause of fear, but
a love of the known world, and the comforts and securities it
provides, is. When the outside world doesn't match or rein-
force the comforts and securities we are used to, the result is
often fear. The fork in the road is whether we seek to replicate
the comfort by other means—new friends, new family, or by
surrounding ourselves with emblems of our prior security in
order to quell the fear. It comes down to whether we address
the fear head-on, dealing with the composition and disman-
tling of it one logical step at a time.

Children have relatively few fears. Many if not most fears
are learned—some version of the big, bad world with its oper-
ative ingredients is imparted in some way, often by mom and
dad. Some fears are innate to the individual. It is as if each person has a built-in understanding that, given the right circumstances, the rug of security can be pulled from under our lives.

The biggest comfort in the midst of fear for a child is knowing he or she will soon be back home—back to mom or dad
and in a place where safety and security are the default setting,
bringing everything else into proper focus. Being in insecure
positions for extended periods of time only makes the heart
long for a return to safety. Think about small children and
their associations with a stuffed bear, a blanket, a certain toy
or pillow. Something needs to be reliable; something needs to
be safe.

When the pendulum swings away from fear—it should

swing to trust in God, but the mark is missed—and pride and self-reliance emerge. The adage of "white-knuckling" a situation—a person grits through a difficult scenario—is pride. It is somewhat like riding the roller coaster of life, gripping the bar while the coaster barrels along at seventy miles per hour. The gripping does nothing if the coaster leaves the tracks, save to solidify that the individual goes down as one with the coaster. The act of gripping simply quiets that inside voice of fear—as if a person can control something external to themselves by exerting physical influence over their surroundings. No, the godly reaction to fear is to find calm and peace, a place where we process the factors of fear with the knowledge that there is something greater to win over our fears, whether it's a trip home to mom and dad or simply securing in our minds the knowledge that the discomfort is temporary.

> The act of gripping simply quiets that inside voice of fear—as if a person can control something external to themselves by exerting physical influence over their surroundings.

Once Judas grew enough to be conscious of himself and his surroundings, the underlying foundation of fears began to root itself in his actions. In an injury on the farm, he cut himself badly as a part of trying to prove his worth to his father, to squash the fear of being insufficient for the work. Each son's initial beacon is his dad, and Judas acted to thwart the imagined burden of proof set before him. Judas had his dark friend fear to thank. He could have feared reprisal for asking too many questions since he knew he had been instructed in how to properly use a saw. He could have feared the sharp response of stress, knowing the family was under obligation to process the olive crop as quickly and efficiently as possible. Whatever the reason, fear held him steady on a course of self-reliance, and the consequences came quickly.

Later, fear of being confronted by the other eleven apostles set Judas's sail toward the noose. He would attempt to throw up a white flag by returning the money he had agreed to from the priests, but the resulting snickering from the teachers of the law only drove his stakes home deeper. Judas was doomed, fear fed adrenaline, and it pushed him to remove himself from the planet rather than face his new, overwhelming reality.

Living reactively is a telltale sign of fear. Sealing off from reality is the zenith of fear, and the largest beacon of the troubled mind, which often heads straight to shame and depression.

Jennifer

I've known Jennifer for years. She had a normal childhood with loving parents and a little brother. In her early years she was building a foundation for a secure life, with a working dad, loving mom, and a home with a swing set and a friend next door. But when Jennifer was just eight, her dad got into an accident and didn't come home. He died, tragically, while saving another man's life. The heroism of that scene was lost on a little girl whose foundation quickly crumbled around her.

Within a few weeks, Jennifer's mom had a new boyfriend. Along with the new man, alcohol would soon find its way into their home. What was once a tranquil home now festered with partying, unpredictability, and the constant fear of what would happen next. Within a year, their family would move away from their home and extended family to start over from scratch and be raised among virtual strangers. While living with this alcoholic boyfriend, in the wilderness no less, and with her mom working, the boyfriend would exert his twisted will, with demeaning chores, mental abuse, and regularly driving drunk with Jennifer and her brother in the car, showing little regard for their well-being. Every day, Jennifer says, seemed an exercise in fear management. But in spite of the changes and jarring experiences, Jennifer was able to make many new friends and thrive where she was, quite a feat given her circumstances. Then again, children often prove amazingly resilient.

As the alcoholism progressed, the stepfather became all the more unpredictable, moving from job to job when he could. He would substitute spankings, threats, teasings, and harsh correction for good parenting. Every time his truck would rumble down the road toward home, the questions went through Jennifer's mind: How much did he drink today before driving home from work? What mood will he be in? It became a strange experience for her to go to sleepovers, where families were normal, no one was scary, and she could escape her reality, even if just for a while. Some days were OK at home, others were like walking on eggshells.

One night when Jennifer was in her tweens, her stepfather got drunk and molested her. Every day after that was a living hell for her: abiding in silence in the same home as her molester, afraid to speak out, afraid to be alone with him. Perhaps worse, Jennifer was afraid what her mother would think if she told her what he was like when she wasn't around. It was a classic trap; unfortunately, far too many children in far too many cultures experience it.

As the years passed and Jennifer's mom finally sought a divorce, the inevitable custody proceedings ensued. Jennifer was grown now, but she had a reason to overcome her fear: she had a little sister. She was determined that her sister not share the same fate. Jennifer found herself facing the task of going to court and testifying to the abuse she had suffered at the man's hands. She sat in a waiting room by herself, waiting to be called into the courtroom. Alone in the midst of strangers, Jennifer faced her abuser, forced to drudge up memories she had fought so hard to repress and move on from. But she faced her fear and overcame.

Jennifer moved on. She moved around the U.S., as a matter of fact. After some travel and a couple of jobs, she met up with what she thought was a great guy. They built a solid relationship. He ran motels and gave her a job. Then one day Jennifer discovered listening devices throughout their home. He had secretly been tapping into her conversations purely out of his own insecurity. Jennifer was attempting to build a new foundation with a new scorecard, but once again someone she trusted and counted on had turned out to be hiding an agenda she knew nothing about, deeply eroding her attempts to rebuild trust and overcome fear.

Still later, Jennifer would attempt to rebuild again. Her resilience was astounding, and yet would face more tests. Her new life in a new state held great promise. Jennifer found love and married. It was finally time to rest and build a life. But then she began to sense that . . . something was amiss. This man too had a second life—another woman—and Jennifer's worst fears came true once again. But Jennifer stayed in that town; she did not leave the area after this latest relationship ended. Someone in Jennifer's shoes may never have trusted again, never ventured past fear to love again. But something in Jennifer pushed her forward.

Each time she needed to remove herself mentally and even geographically from harmful people and memories, Jennifer found ways, including through counseling, to renew her zeal for life. She learned about space, she learned about boundaries, she learned about her own value. She *learned*. Jennifer is now a successful teacher and mentor in a large city, where she helps kids, some of whom face abuse themselves. She gives them a leg up when life has eroded their foundations. Today she is happily married and has a son she loves dearly.

It took Jennifer years of counseling and healing. I will never forget a conversation I had with her about all she had been through. She confided in me: "I am *not* these things. I am not a victim. I am a survivor."

It is amazing to think what can be accomplished in the face of fear. It is also amazing to think about the decisions we make based on fear, and even worse, at times, the decisions we delay or refuse to make based on those same fears. Abuse from loved ones, scorn from classmates, failing in a public arena—there are many entryways for fear to enter and grip our lives. Whether a simple fear of a roller coaster, fear of public places, certain people groups—you name it. Much of life goes unexplored, unconquered, or unenjoyed, all because fear takes the place of desire, joy, or energy itself.

> She confided in me: "I am *not* these things. I am not a victim. I am a survivor."

A popular T-shirt these days reads: "Introverts unite! Separately, in our own homes." I have a friend whose wife is afraid of practically everything. Her mind destroys a suggestion with what-if questions and all the reasons something *can't* happen. A simple request like, "Can you take our daughter to the dentist?" is met with a gauntlet of excuses: work schedule, her dentistry isn't that urgent, there's no time, or others. She is afraid of engagement with her own child! Unbridled fear in our minds can be crippling to the very people we care about the most. And yet, we all do this in varying degrees.

Sometimes there is a genuine phobia or genuine emotion of feeling sad or down, and the fear of activity outside our normal selves can be daunting. But many times the true reason for not being honest or engaged isn't that we don't have time to do something with someone—it is a fear of relationship and commitment. We have been hurt, and so we believe that the next person will treat us just like the previous ones did.

We can take Jennifer's sterling example as fuel to never stop trying, to never give up, to push past present circumstances.

Are you a slave to fear? In what capacity? What do you use to get past the fear or fears? Have you resolved to not change anything in your life because you have justified a level of satisfaction with yourself? Is it fear that stops you from pushing into unchartered territory? Do something new, different. The challenge is to never stop exploring. Live life to the full! How will you take the next step?

THE REASON

In his mind, Judas was pleased to attempt a merger of sorts between the priesthood and the ranks of Jesus and the twelve. In the public eye, Jesus fit the priesthood in stature. Judas determined that there was still a chance to prove his worth, to be as significant as the others. He would use his leverage and knowledge of the priestly system and couple that with Jesus' command of the crowds. There was no question Jesus had the following. There was no question he had the teaching. And there was absolutely no question he carried the authority. In fact, he had acquired great amounts of authority.

In truth, Jesus was no longer on any level of par with the teachers of the law—he had surpassed them. After all, when pushed, the teachers could not match his knowledge or Scripture application, and they always left his discussions puzzled, frustrated, or both. Because of this, it was troublesome for Judas to work this relationship between the powerful priesthood and Jesus, but he thought the situation workable if he could get the circumstances right. Hillel might be on to something.

However, in the other part of his intellect, Judas saw a problem. He knew he could not move Jesus to act differently. If he could just get Jesus to back off a bit, and help fasten upon the politically possessed religious leaders the understanding that Jesus really was harmless, this tension could be relieved for all of them.

Jesus was truly a problem. Judas had a strange draw to him, but the feelings he had inside did not, at the same time, sit well with that draw. The early yearning he had to run, to be near, even to crawl under crowds—the wonder of Jesus!—had been replaced by suspicion and a smoldering anger. It wasn't that Judas was going to ask Jesus to tone it down. He knew better. He understood his teacher more than he let on. He had been disciplined by his rabbi. He had been trained, and he understood. It made him sick to his stomach, and as he thought it over, he literally shook his head in an attempt to shake off the thought. There was an attempt within Judas to dissuade himself from his path. But he had chosen, he had decided: this way—his way—was better. It had to be. It was the way that Judas *needed*, because Judas needed satisfaction. He needed significance. There was no way he had taken the gamble of leaving the grove to simply learn from yet another teacher and carry his money. Judas had a destiny to fulfill: to fix the Jewish nation in his time. Jesus' way just wouldn't work.

The Jewish leaders brought their own insecurities to a boil, and these were creating a huge amount of stress everywhere the disciples ventured. It was not, at that point, a measure of whether what Jesus said was truth, but whether these men could share the spotlight.

Jesus was—in some ways, literally (witness the scene in the temple courts)—upsetting the apple cart. The Jewish leaders had spent considerable time forming and manipulating a position for themselves. Judas was hoping for a middle ground, one in which he could continue with Jesus, maintain his relationship with Hillel, and distance himself from potential shame within the ranks of the Council and from his own family. To quell the hatred among the leadership for his master by using political appeasement—this would be the way.

Judas had succeeded in satisfying his yearning to fill the void in a friendship that had been carried but left unfed. Hillel had given Judas a satisfying release in his life, a reason to look forward to another day. Judas did not want to leave his new friend disappointed. Hillel represented a place to forget his troubles and a place, perhaps, even to laugh, a place Judas still needed.

Judas knew there had been a turning of events inside himself. He was listening to his own voice now. He saw, through his own industriousness, an opportunity to make a difference—just as his father had taught him. But his difference was self-motivated, self-appreciating, and self-fulfilling. He would not be a mender of branches for his family's well-being, he would be an agent for the joining of the truth of the gospel with the power of Jewish influence.

Judas was desperate for attention, for significance. He knew who he was; he knew what he was capable of. Many a lesson from his father was ringing true now; Judas had blossomed, he was sure, and understood so much. At the same time, the pruning he had done with his father now seemed a distant memory. He now saw the branches that he would be mending as vines of the Jewish faith. Jesus had come to prune, to help the tree of God bear the fruit it was supposed to. Judas saw that clearly now. More importantly to him, he saw his role in this drama.

Jesus, Judas believed, just did not have the skill set to graft this freshly pruned movement back into the religious order that ruled. Judas knew what was being passed by when Jesus did not give him the opportunities he thought he deserved. Judas was an asset, untapped by Jesus, and this decision was costing the Jews their place, their standing with the Romans, and ultimately a much closer connection with God.

Judas knew that Jesus was to supplant the Jewish nation. Judas was concerned that he had worked too hard to understand this world of men, culture, and religion—and that would all be spoiled by Jesus' changes. Judas was not about to let it be torn apart before he could work the situation. The Jews needed someone who understood the times, who knew the political climate, who could give them the nation they desired. They did not need to be overthrown—by voice or by force.

They simply needed unity. They needed Judas.

It was a matter of wisdom. The people, the Jews, were uncomprehending of the matters unfolding around them. To be a leader, you had to make decisions like a king, rule like a king would, and represent God. Judas's appetite for significance had been so turned into a froth that he scarcely could stand it. His thoughts were processing faster now, his mood fueled by the understanding of who he was

> Judas's appetite for significance had been so turned into a froth that he scarcely could stand it.

to be and what his life mission was becoming. If there was anger, it was being concealed by drive, ambition, determination.

Once Jesus revealed his power in front of the Council, there would be no stopping them. Judas would navigate the intricacies of the Council, and after Jesus presented himself, confirming their suspicions, Judas would be the one to step in, to interpret the truth for these men to understand. He would forge a peace that would profit all Israel.

The other apostles saw how important it was to be guided by wisdom, to be ruled by the principles of old. They intended to bring to fruition, with Jesus' power and drive, the culmination of everything they had heard men speak of. The Kingdom of God was indeed upon them.

Octavian, with his so-called insurrectionists and revolutionaries, would have no choice but to follow. Jesus had already silenced the many so-called prophets—those fueled by themselves for themselves—and they would now see what was possible when God was actually with them. Judas was sure that Jesus was going to thank him. Judas would force the issue. He would use Jesus to show the world what God was all about. He would get Jesus to talk to the men of the Council in power.

It was a perfect plan. For some reason, Judas's fists were clenched. It was a matter of compulsion. On the one hand, Jesus had once been everything to Judas. Jesus had helped Judas blossom more than he would realize. But it was the weeds in his heart growing alongside the good soil that choked him. Now Jesus was no longer a hero or mentor. He was no longer the one who had chosen him, who sought to love and groom him.

Judas, in his youth, had been much needier than he let on. His utter dependence on attention and appreciation had been stifled for years as a menial worker on a farm. Simon had been working to build a legacy, and in so doing he'd forgotten to build his son. The love bred into young Judas's heart by his mother had been quashed by the duties brought by being the distant son of an entrepreneur.

There are many lessons for a young man to learn, but the hardest lesson is one not taught: you will miss your father when you leave. Judas was not privileged to have learned this. He learned tasks, he learned a trade. He did not learn the tears of a father carrying his bleeding son home. Judas did not learn care when he was berated with impatience when he left good olives squashed beneath his feet. There was no time for feeling; there was no room for anything except the duties of a firstborn son. So he did not learn the deeper lessons. There was not time. There was no good-bye hug, no meaningful handshake of acknowledgement. The bar mitzvah given for him was mandatory, unfeeling—it had only meant so much. He may have become accountable to God in men's eyes that day, but in Judas's eyes he was still seeking to please the man who had essentially driven him away.

Indeed, the fruit had been plucked too soon to ripen.

In all his toil, there was never a thank you from his father. There were only tasks, duties, the preparation for another day. Every ounce of his energy had been poured into the grove. It would be true to say that Judas actually poured forth his labor not to see olives grow, not to help provide for his family, but in an attempt, with every pruning, to harvest adoration and approval from his father.

To what end is it to toil when men forget their roots—the very things they are attempting to build, fortify, and nourish? Judas would have none of it; there was no talk, no thought, and no appreciation for what had been done for him. When he thought of home, there was bitterness more than anything else. Surely he must now be seen as one who would not complete a task, one who had no honor, one who was unworthy to inherit what he did not appreciate.

He would be no heir; he would make no lasting impression on the community by carrying the family burden. No, Judas would be making his mark under Jesus of Nazareth. Jesus would pay for the unmaking of his manhood. He had counted on Jesus, as had his family, to continue to train him, to mold him into a man.

Judas would take back his life; he would make it count. What Simon Iscariot could not do in the training of his son, Judas would complete on his own.

So the burden lay on Jesus to fulfill what his father had not. And now, in Judas's eyes, Jesus had failed him as well. The lessons were not tailored to Judas's needs . . . or, perhaps they were. It was just that Judas was not ready to hear them. So a legacy of training and manhood fell to the ground somewhere between father and son. Another legacy, one of discipleship, fell somewhere between Jesus and his student.

This was the middle ground of a young man who was to leave both legacies unfulfilled. In doing so he would seal his fate and, in one sense, that of his rabbi as well.

THE FIGHT

It wasn't cold outside. In fact, it was quite mild. The sun set a bit early this time of year, so when it turned to the ninth hour, the only street glow belonged to the lamps left burning in a few shop windows. It was rather serene, and desperately lonely.

Judas was cold. He had just left a meeting that was to be a fulfillment of the prophecy in his mind, a prophecy to fix a nation of people, secure God's favor, and bring his naive vision of a unified leadership of God's people to fruition. He had been blind to himself and blind to the reality surrounding him. What Judas failed to realize was the amount of callousness that had gripped his heart over the past several months. It grew from the seeds of his discontent and blossomed into the hardest bark of a tree, attempting to protect the tenderness within. In its protection of his pain, hurt, and anger, it strangled out logic, suffocated hope, and left trust twisting in the wind.

Now, somehow, it was gone. The gentle, understanding voices of the priests tore the callous shield off his bosom with their flattery, revealing its fruit: a hard, cynical heart. And it was cold. Judas looked around, realizing that returning to the others was impossible. Not only was he paranoid that they would know, but something else stopped him. He knew he had acted in secret, he knew the others would not understand, and he knew Jesus *would know*. It was too much. He started to feel guilty. The callousness he had nurtured for so long had shielded his heart from the pounding reality of friendly voices, from the spiritual truth trying to free his mind from its own trap.

He knew he had acted in secret, he knew the others would not understand, and he knew Jesus *would know*.

Never mind all that. Judas was not surrendered to the waiting period between his plan and its execution. His reality was crushing him from all sides, the reality that he had betrayed innocence, betrayed trust. He wasn't ready for the insecurity and the squirming and the doubts that would come between his plan to unify the Jews and the meeting that would be the catalyst.

There were no doubts in his mind when he started. His preoccupation with thoughts and visions of what could be, what would be, clouded the fatal mistakes he was making. He thought it was a flawless plan, and now he was quickly realizing his vision and plan were nothing like those of the Pharisees and councilmen.

That might have been just as well, but there was a larger problem for Judas. In his heart of hearts, if he had been honest, he would have known from the beginning that they had a different plan than he did. Honesty was another casualty left bleeding alongside his path to significance. If Judas were honest with himself, he would have exchanged their recent smiles with the more steady visions he had in his memory—visions of their whispering, their scheming, their dark side. A side Jesus had warned all of them about, a side Judas had chosen to befriend rather than protect against. His pride told him he could compete with, understand, and foil their schemes with his own plan, his own determination, his own significance.

> They didn't ask anything further of his plans, they just asked—again— about the exact location of the group. All they really wanted was Jesus.

When he met with them, his words delivered themselves not as a grand plan for Israel, but as a weak sales pitch, something like selling rancid olive oil. It was nothing like his father's pitch for the olive grove so long ago, he would think. He could see it: when he told the Council his plan, they smiled and thanked him for his information. The meeting that started with smiles had turned serious, and the smile left Judas's face as quickly as it sprang up. He was learning the way men schemed and planned, and he was learning that intentions were everything. It was an ugly moment. It revealed the true nature of the situation: Judas wanted to be heard, he wanted to matter. They didn't ask anything further of his plans, they just asked—again—about the exact location of the group. All they really wanted was Jesus.

What stung was that his voice, his information, his vision— all of it fell on deaf ears. They heard exactly what they wanted, and they were done. Judas left that meeting still convinced he had acted in accordance with what was right. But this was a battle he would lose. His thoughts betrayed him in every instance. Every place his eyes looked he saw shadows, not light. He didn't know what he felt, but he knew one thing: he was alone.

No matter the circumstances, no matter how he tried and tried to justify it all away, Judas knew he was no longer as important as he had been when the meeting with the priests had started. No matter how much he wanted to be right in his eyes, his family's eyes, and even to God, he was wrong and now he knew it. How could this be? How could he have ended up on the wrong side of history? On the wrong side of the one issue that mattered to him most?

> Judas knew he was no longer as important as he had been when the meeting with the priests had started.

He would never forget the look in Jesus' eyes earlier that night. Jesus had handed Judas the bread, and Jesus knew. Jesus always knew.

Judas panicked.

The desire to be important was like breathing. The compulsion was too strong. Like a child when he sees a stick of cinnamon, or a boy who spies something shiny in the creek bottom. He has to know what it is. He has to get his shoes wet, he *has* to retrieve it. *It will be worth it once everyone sees what I've found*, he thinks in his heart. Judas had to turn Jesus over. He had to fulfill his need to be important. And Jesus needed to be stopped. The constant badgering, teaching, telling people what was needed in everything in their lives. Sure, there were miracles, and there certainly was wisdom, but this was getting out of hand. People were trying to make him their king, and Judas was tired of it all. To Judas, Jesus' trajectory was an unsustainable path; it was too good to be true.

How Jesus did things seemed sneaky and divine all at the

same time, and it drove Judas to the edge. In his mind he had become "the man in between," in between those who stood for what was right and those who stood for what was established. He was a pioneer in misery, he realized, and he did not like it.

The money was jangling in his purse. He hated it. He had become part of a system. There was a piece of security in the coins, the "reward"—the weight itself had a nice feel. Judas began to spend the money in his mind. Just as his eyes saw shadows rather than figures, so his thoughts of spending saw only dark things. Insurrectionists could be bought, he began to think, to help in the overthrow of the Romans from Jerusalem. But such a move would scarcely be enough to make a dent, if he were honest. He was only dreaming now, fooling himself into believing he really had a plan. The shadow of the money being spent on Judas's vision for a unified Jerusalem wasn't a drop in the bucket. He had no backing, no momentum, no companions. What was worse, and what was crashing down on him now, was the realization that he had no heart or intention of following through. From start to finish, Judas Iscariot had

> He was nothing more than a scared young man in way over his head. Not an apostle, but the fruit of living as a casual disciple.

captained a dream, but he had left it at the dock. He started to panic. Adrenaline was pumping now. His eyes opened again, and he saw what Jesus and the others knew: he was nothing more than a scared young man in way over his head. Not an apostle, but the fruit of living as a casual disciple.

He had only a single recourse. He had to return the money. He had to explain that Jesus was innocent, that he, Judas, was actually the guilty one, and that the misunderstanding needed cleared. But it was too late. He had given permission to these men to launch their plan, one that had been laid out carefully, precisely, deliberately, professionally. The magnitude of the coming event now swarmed and engulfed Judas.

The shadow spoke deep in his mind. He hadn't worked a plan to make his vision a reality because he didn't believe it himself. It was all simply a parading of thoughts, a tantalizing daydream. He had no intentions, no true plan, and no fuel for any of it. He had wrecked something for no reason other than self-pity.

His attempt to restore order to his circumstance—his tossing the money bag to the priests, and his few words along with it—was short-lived. The priests simply laughed at him, shrugged him off, sent him back to his living nightmare. There would be no reversal of fortune; the course was set, and Judas was the guide. They commanded him to lead them to the garden where the disciples would be gathered together. Now he felt sick. He could not escape his fate, so he followed through with their plan. Jesus and the others were just where Judas had anticipated. All the men watched his betrayal when he kissed Jesus in the garden. It was the worst moment of his life.

> His attempt to restore order to his circumstance—his tossing the money bag to the priests, and his few words along with it— was short-lived. The priests simply laughed at him.

He started walking, now alone. He was quick at first, but he slowed down as his mind wandered through the memory of what just happened. He was making his way out of Jerusalem without intending to do so. It was too tricky a place, and he was suddenly yearning to be home. *Somewhere safe.* He was acting as a child now, the laughingstock of the other kids. He was wounded and confused, and the only thing that kept him from diving headlong into insanity was to keep walking.

His family had been proud of him, to a degree. Their son had latched onto the faith. They didn't really know the extent of the damage Jesus had done to the Jewish religion they loved, or would do once his mission was complete, but they were happy that the perceived anger in their son had left. He had been able to visit them on several occasions, and they noted in him a marked amount of maturity, as if years had been added to his life. He was the new pride of his clan, and his siblings looked to him more than ever. At times, he even found himself imitating Jesus: he would hold his young sisters on his lap, patting their heads, encouraging them.

Judas didn't dare think of all of them at this time. He was trying to reconcile the happenings in his mind. He was grateful that Jerusalem stood some six miles from his hometown. He needed time to think, he needed time to reason. The news of what was transpiring around him would not beat him home. He would have the first chance to explain. His family didn't understand the intricacies of the situation at hand, and Judas would bring them to light. This battle, he would win. The Pharisees would not be speaking for him, he would have a chance to do that. But then he remembered . . . he didn't really believe in it after all. He was just a mixed-up, perplexed young man who had gotten too big for his britches.

The more he walked, the more he realized he would not just have to explain, he would have to confess. The panic from the disciples that he had set in motion was a silent wave that crashed around him. He began to run. He needed to get away from the world. It had crushed him, it was rubbing his face in the dirt. His fists were clenched. He was angry again, only this time the object of his wrath was himself. He stopped. It was very late now, and the night was dark.

He passed centurions on the road, each of them inquiring what he was doing and urging him to either turn back or get home. He decided to chance it on the side trails. He couldn't be around people anymore. He knew he could be robbed and was glad he had gotten rid of the silver, but wary that his only means of bartering with a band of thieves was gone. He risked being murdered, and the more he thought about that, the more he welcomed the possibility. It would be a great escape. If he were gone he wouldn't have to deal with the explanations he would owe his family for returning home, and he would never have to deal with the problem of returning to Jerusalem and running into one of the disciples.

But that night, under a full moonlight, there were no murderers to be found to bail him out of his trouble. It was cold. Judas, despite all that earlier adrenaline, had run out of energy. He stopped to sleep under a bush. Maybe, just maybe, he would be bitten by a snake, or perhaps a boar might attack. His mind was bent on destroying himself. The callousness had returned, and it was even thicker now. He was actively plotting his own demise. The stinging self-awareness was ugly. He was glad there were no lakes for reflections to be seen.

He remembered how he had cut himself while pruning. He remembered the uneasy feeling he had at that time; he had that same emotion now. He slept for what seemed like fifteen minutes, but it was actually a few hours.

He got up and resolutely set out for home.

19

ON GUILT

"No guilt is forgotten so long as the conscience still knows of it."
—Stefan Zweig[5]

The hollow pit in the stomach. That is guilt. Usually people don't "feel guilty" until someone calls them on it, or they wake from their deed to the voice of their conscience. I was taught long ago that guilt isn't a feeling. It is a state of being. We either *are* guilty or we are *not* guilty. It is, of itself, clinical. The "feeling" in the state of guilt is actually along the lines of sadness or shame. I for one understand this completely, having spent a bit too much time in front of judges pleading "no contest" to charges brought against me in my youthful, idiotic days.

> Usually people don't "feel guilty" until someone calls them on it, or they wake from their deed to the voice of their conscience.

Pleading no contest was a way of saying, "I really don't want to drudge up the past, your Honor. Let's just acknowledge that I'm here, and I don't want to be here, and you just go ahead and give me whatever sentence you're going to give me." Legally, "no contest" means the defendant isn't going to bother contesting the charges against him (or her); the judge is free to pass sentence. It's a fancy way of saying "I did it" without admitting guilt, without totally revisiting the hollow pit in the stomach.

When the judge said, "The people against Steve Jordan," it sent chills down my spine. Walking into court and seeing my mother there—an extreme ouch. But the sense of genuine guilt began to manifest when I was taken to jail. Or when I was putting on orange reflective vests and picking up trash around the courthouse. When people saw me physically incarcerated and I couldn't play it off like, "I'm just walking around here, doing my thing with a trash claw in my hand and a bucket." It began when I realized, as recovery circles teach, that "my best thinking got me here." It is in these moments the sense of guilt arrives in force. When the information registers in the brain that an action was indeed my fault—that is when the state of guilt kicks in. It does take on a feeling, one that sticks something like Velcro. Because, even though, in a clinical sense, I was in a state of guilt and convicted of a crime, it was me we were talking about, and it was very embarrassing, saddening, and many other emotions. It was the child inside my mind, speaking to me words I didn't want to hear, but words I needed to hear: *Steve, what are you doing here? Is this the best you could do? Seriously?*

Those whispers are the catalyst for true understanding of perhaps every wrong we commit against ourselves or others. When the voice inside your head gets hold of you when you make a mistake, is it a gentle, corrective voice—something like Jesus walking beside you, placing his arm around you, speaking to you? Or is it a harsh tone? *See what you did? You're worthless, you're an idiot, now we're here again, the same old thing!* This is important to recognize, because whatever that voice tells us—how it talks to us—represents the depth and length we will have the sense of guilt hanging over us.

It's not criminal to have a sense of guilt. It's just accurate. When we don't make mistakes and yet still feel guilty, that's not actually "feeling guilty"—that's shame we put on ourselves, or the shame-recording we have heard through our lives and experiences, reminding us that perhaps we didn't do something wrong, but if we could have, we probably would have. And that is something different.

A very real question begs: How long is guilt supposed to "survive" in us? From a technical standpoint, we are all guilty; we have all violated our conscience at some point. But are we still supposed to hang our heads because we stole candy when we were five? If that was the case, we wouldn't be hanging our heads, we'd be crawling on the ground—if we could even move—from the weight of all the guilt we'd be carrying.

Hugs All Around

It's interesting when my young kids "get in trouble." There is an immediate cloud in the room. Their little world suddenly has a spotlight, and they know it. Enter parental tone and eye-level talk.

"What happened?"

"I hit Marie."

"Why did you hit her?"

"I wanted her toy and she wouldn't give it to me."

"We use words. We don't hit, do we?"

"No."

Insert image of quivering lip.

"Go sit on your bed in timeout after you apologize to Marie."

"OK." Tears. Rubbing of the eyes. "Now can I have a hug?"

The broken child is immediately sorry, starts crying, and wants a hug. The conversation may not go that well all the time, but the result is always the same: the child wants restored and reaffirmed that, though she made a mistake, she is *still* loved. That's a pretty big deal, and it has taught me a lot about dealing with and handling guilt. The person's closure on a given matter is tied to being restored to a state of acceptance in spite of the guilt.

The State of Ohio was relatively easy. The scorecard of restoration came when I did my time, got my license back, performed community service, fulfilled probation for a year, paid the fine, and went to an intervention program. I could tell the judge wasn't too impressed with me. I got the entire kitchen sink. After all that, even with paying my debt to society, I still often would get a quickened pulse when I saw a police officer. I may have gotten square with the State of Ohio, but it has literally taken years for me to not still feel a sense of guilt when I pass a police car on the road. Maybe I should have asked the judge for a hug.

> The person's closure on a given matter is tied to being restored to a state of acceptance in spite of the guilt.

Either way, there is a reconciliation we aim for in processing wrongs involving people. Some guilt is absolved by sharing a conversation, an apology, a good laugh. Indeed, one can gauge how dysfunctional—or functional—a relationship is by the methodology used in amending wrongs. It used to be that my friends and I would get drunk or high to fix our relationship issues. That rhymes with dysfunctional! Another way of seeing this: think about dogs. It's funny how they relate to people after they've been scolded for doing something wrong. They can't wait until life is back to normal with their owner again. They are so eager to be restored. But they are nonetheless mindful of their transgression.

Internally, the length of time we torture ourselves over wrongdoing is a direct reflection of two things: Our view of self (remember the self-talk when we have gotten ourselves into a bad situation); and the value we place on others' views of us. We either see our worth, or the lack of it. We change course when we acknowledge the need to march on with life and move beyond the knowledge that we've slipped up.

Sports aficionados call this "quarterback memory." When a quarterback is guilty of throwing an interception—especially at a crucial moment in a game—he knows that once the other side has made his team pay the penalty for the error, he has to go right back onto that field and once again sling the ball around, risking another interception. He has to forgive himself or he will fall apart under the pressure. He understands one crucial thing: mistakes are part of the game. Television directors and cameramen love to focus on the guilty quarterback as the other team takes the ball down the field and scores off the turnover. Directors are sadistic in that way. It seems that redemption for the quarterback only comes if the team turns it around and wins the game—as if the quarterback has no life or worth outside the game! Fortunately for most athletes, a decent balance in life keeps things in perspective.

Judas, like most young people, had difficulty with perspective. He possessed little in life experience from which to draw. We'll never know if he thought through the possibility of rejoining the other apostles. Judas had to be able to find a way toward forgiveness, and it turns out that path wasn't one he could walk. The irony for Judas was that he watched Jesus literally forgive people's sins—many times. "Move on now and sin no more," Jesus would essentially tell those people. It makes one wonder if Judas really believed the words when he heard them. Could Jesus *actually* forgive sin? Who would know, anyway? After all, the real scorecard is not on a public billboard perched above someone's head. Judas perhaps understood that there was a difference in being forgiven by Jesus for a sin against others, but this was actually a sin against the forgiver himself. It was unchartered territory, perhaps, but as things escalated, Judas soon realized the magnitude of what he had done, and thus the magnitude of his guilt. For Judas, the depth and enormity of his betrayal made walking the path toward forgiveness an impossibility. What human could possibly stand up to the knowledge that they had been the catalyst for the death of the Son of God? Somewhere, somehow Judas would have had to count on Jesus' teachings being deeply embedded in someone's heart to forgive him, at least on a human level. But that's tough sledding.

> For Judas, the depth and enormity of his betrayal made walking the path toward forgiveness an impossibility.

Here's where it gets sticky. People want to let Judas off the hook. So he was doomed to destruction. When Jesus dipped the bread in the bowl, the apostle John tells us that Satan "entered into" Judas. Once the task of betrayal was accomplished, it could be said that Satan released Judas, because Judas later confessed in one very real sense. He was "seized with remorse," Scripture says. Since Judas couldn't walk that path toward forgiveness in spite of his guilt, his fate of being doomed to final destruction was, it seems, sealed. The guilt proved too much to bear, too much to live with. His guilt would graduate to shame in short order, and he would end his life.

Greg

I have known Greg for years. Greg was an up-and-coming minister in a church he loved dearly. Though he was busy with ministry work from dawn until the wee hours on most nights, and spent countless hours in meetings and workshops, he had holes in his life. He grew up uncertain of who he really was; he had little encouragement in a broken home. He thought himself destined for ministry, having been converted in his twenties and having received so many answers to questions no one in his life could give.

Greg married, had children, and had a solid life laid out for himself. He had a congregation that loved him, friends everywhere he turned, and a supportive family—the sky was the limit. But his unhealthy past, growing up around drugs, alcohol, and promiscuity, would not leave him alone. He was dutiful as a Christian, to be sure, confessing his heart attitudes and sins, repenting as much as he knew how. But he could not shake his past. He spiraled into a world of sin with pornography, guilt, and shame. He would lose his ministry job; he would be publically challenged on his attitudes and actions with women he worked with and encountered. It seemed he was a caged animal that had come unbound.

His cheating heart ended up fulfilling itself with another woman. Greg would be forced to own his mistakes, and he scarred his marriage, his kids, and changed the trajectory of his family's future. His only saving grace was his wife. She had been living a faithful life, following the lead of her husband, proud of his accomplishments, loving the ways he would teach, counsel, and help church members of all ages. Even as he began battling his addiction, she wavered, but she would never lose her honor and trust in the man who she said "I do" to so many years before.

Greg attended group meetings, put pen to paper to chronicle his repentance, and slowly began to piece his life together. It was hard work, because as anyone will tell you when a person enters counseling, Greg was digging into his past, attempting to fill the holes in his mind and heart while simultaneously living in the present. He still had to conquer, on a daily basis, the coldness of his home, the challenges of his family, and the task of fulfilling his duties as a provider in spite of his challenges. Perhaps the greatest task of all was the knowledge that he was the cause of so much destruction and discord. He had guilt all over him. He could no longer attend his old church. The relationships, the trust—it was all fractured. With the collateral damage, Greg couldn't shake the guilt, even amid the changes he had made. Even amid the forgiveness he was given. Even years later, he had the look of a man still guilty.

> With the collateral damage, Greg couldn't shake the guilt, even amid the changes he had made.

People see others who struggle with addiction and they notice a *look* in the addicted person's eyes. It's actually a question, or questions, the struggling person wants answered: "Do you know about me? Are you judging me? Will you talk to me like I'm *that guy*? Do you forgive me? Do you know my wife forgives me? Do you know I'm working on me?" Dealing with marriage as God intended is more of a challenge now than it ever has been. The acceptance and commonality of divorce and remarriage, let alone the massive temptations offered through technology, make today's atmosphere overwhelming to the unprepared. The proverbial "scarlet letter" that had previously been reserved for women is now more accurately attributed to men, who must deal with their own guilt and shame for their actions. Those who know the mentality faced by men in this area know exactly the look men give each other who are struggling. "The eyes are the lamp of the body," Jesus said. Men who are asking the same questions Greg asks are actually asking that question about themselves: *Am I that guy? Do I forgive myself? Am I judging me? Do I know I am forgiven? Do I live like it?*

Many times people want to call these episodes "shame." Many times the biggest difference with being in a state of guilt and one of feeling shame is that those who are guilty have actually done something to deserve the reality they are living in. That reality may be a sad state of affairs, whether by marital separation, child visitation conflicts, divorce, job loss, public ridicule. There are many fallen dominoes as a result of our actions, but the new reality doesn't constitute a *continual* state of shame and guilt. That lies between the ears of the person at the eye of the hurricane, and also those who are right next to them. Everyone who loves someone has to process their loved one's mistakes. Shame is brought upon an undeserving person many times; guilt is brought upon someone by the actions of that individual—either guilt in the conscience or publicly admitted guilt.

> There are many fallen dominoes as a result of our actions, but the new reality doesn't constitute a *continual* state of shame and guilt.

It can grow and become shame if we do not understand the depth of love the Creator has for us. The true wrestling match for the guilty party is being able to accept the forgiveness of others and, in turn, being able to truly forgive themselves. We can wrestle with being so overcome with our own actions that we perceive our sin as unforgiveable. It is a weird pride that thinks what we have done is too much to forgive—as if something worse hasn't happened in the world. More than likely, in these scenarios, we had a personal scorecard that was set for a hole in one on every single hole, and we can't get over the fact that we three-putted.

Greg shattered his life and yet resurrected it after years of focused change. He would say he has aged twice his years, and yet is somehow renewed. Still, he admits there are times he walks around with his own personal cloud—not because he feels unworthy and shamed about life, but because he still feels guilt for what he has done. Some would say it is a good thing given the severity of what he did: preventative medicine, they might call it. Greg is consistently grateful for his second chances at a life he knew he had train-wrecked. He has told me, however, that dealing with his cloud of guilt is job number one, and he has since committed to "turning off" his self-talk and walking as he should: forgiven and whole.

Is there something in your life you're holding onto in an unhealthy way? Are you "over-guilting" yourself? Remember the quarterback's perseverance. While we know we feel a conscience issue, what happens if we let it rule over our lives? What could be left unaccomplished? Maybe it's time to wrap up the present and toss it for good.

THE SENTENCE

Dawn was breaking as Judas reached the outskirts of town. He looked back down the path—there was nothing but dust and hills. Jerusalem and her anarchy would be far away. He turned back and made his way through the quiet streets. He had finally come home.

Judas saw his sisters' toys outside. He stopped cold. He sat down in front of the house, in the dirt, and cried. He didn't know why; he just cried. The reflection he was afraid of had shown itself. Home was where he was the responsible one, the one the young Iscariot children looked up to, and it was this image that broke him down.

He had failed. He was with a man who did nothing wrong, who attempted to teach him the things missing in his life, and he had betrayed him.

He could no longer be a hero—not even to his siblings. He could not explain this to anyone. What would they say? What would they do? He didn't want to face his father. He certainly didn't want to go back to work at the grove. He saw that as an admission that he couldn't make it in the big city, that he was still young, still a child. It would be a huge step backward, an admission that he was not ready to be significant. He had been graduated into manhood; he was no longer a son with his father. In his mind, he had arrived, but in truth he had arrived too soon. At the same time, he found himself wanting to go back to simpler times, before travel, before the summer at his cousin's. Before Jesus. He would have to be broken in front of the man he wanted to surpass. He couldn't do that.

He remembered his mother, her simple ways. Her singing, her floating around the house while he watched. She would be crushed. Would she understand? Would she see his folly and forgive him? He had to know, but he also couldn't bring himself to tell her that innocence had been betrayed by his hand.

He looked to the side of the house. He wiped the tears from his face. There were tools there, tools that reminded him of being in control. He wielded a saw—the same one he had cut his finger on as a boy. He smiled briefly, shook his head. Then he cried more. He wanted to go back, to tell himself—as a boy—that he didn't need to panic, that it would be alright. His eyes could barely focus. He fumbled through the various items in the shed.

He knew what he was doing there. He had known when he left Jerusalem. It was a game in the back of his mind, a deadly game with one toy. It was his own thoughts that betrayed him. Within his mind, there was a voice. It arrived when he was weakest, when he least expected it. It was a whisper. It was his own voice, but it spoke a language foreign to him. It was the language of utter despair, of final defeat. And now that voice was reaching a crescendo in his mind. It was time to do what the voice was telling him. There truly was no choice. The kids' toys, his very home, had sealed his fate, and now he was following the instructions he heard in his head, the ones that would silence the sorrow. Then he stopped. Gathering whatever steam he had inside, he turned and grabbed the rope. He set out for the grove. By the time he arrived, it was after sunup.

Normally he would find himself, in this place, preparing for harvest with his father. He walked in a trance to the oldest tree, at the edge of the grove by a field, and began the climb. He sat there, on top of a firm, mature branch, for a very long time. The voice was silent now. It had delivered him to this place, dropped him off here to ponder his fate, to test his resolve.

The morning warmed nicely. The birds moved swiftly from tree to tree, gathering supplies and the day's food. Crickets were chirping their usual song. Life was moving. No one knew where he was, which is exactly how he wanted it. He no longer understood himself, what made him do the things he had done. He didn't want to know. He just wanted it to be over.

So he put the rope around his neck and scooted to the edge of the branch. Tears streamed down his face through the stressed and gritted features of anger. He was completely overwhelmed—and completely in control.

He looked over the grove and the field from this vantage point. He actually thought to pray. The mornings were such a serene time. But life was too pressing on him, and much too complicated for prayer.

This was the only way out. He pushed off.

21

ON SHAME

"What is the seal of liberation?
No longer to be ashamed in our own presence."
—Friedrich Nietzsche[6]

Shame is the dark lord over the lives of so many. For some, the manifestation of shame is shown, unfortunately, in the physical presence of a certain individual or even a crowd of them. For others, it is a hint in our minds that grows into a tree, blocking any rays of sun that might illuminate confidence in us. For many more, shame is a voice that looks at normalcy and says, "That could probably never be me."

Give some thought for a moment to the saying, "You should be ashamed of yourself." It's an easy colloquialism for

> Shame is a voice that looks at normalcy and says, "That could probably never be me."

someone to mutter, almost as easy as breathing. Yet we are *not* told when confronted with this statement to be ashamed of our *action*, which is really just galvanized guilt, but instead to be ashamed of *ourselves*. It is as if our very self—our thoughts, heart, mind, and body—is in need of a dark cloud over it for life! It is a classification of the entire person rather than isolating and objectively looking at the wrong or disapproved-of action.

Unless people toe the line of the current societal picture, they are potential subjects to shame. Sometimes it's made very public. In Ohio, for instance, car license plates are yellow for a period of three years when the driver of the vehicle is convicted of drunk driving. It is a device indicating a DUI and/or restricted driving, but it is also a deterrent, and an example of a shaming technique. Some things bring consequences: you misbehave, you go to the principal's office. You do it again? You wear a dunce hat. That's shaming. Other venues for people unloading shame are via social media (keyboard warriors unite!), the news (from the caught-on-camera stuff all the way to the anchor's tone of voice), the schoolroom (we've all seen bullying), and the workplace (bosses who thrive on poor management techniques; one can picture Alec Baldwin in *Glengarry Glen Ross*).

It is true that, when we mess up, we should be ashamed of our actions, but to recast our *entire* being into a hellish prison of self-doubt and to be ashamed of our very selves is a bit much. But that is what we do, and coercive people, online forums, or groups of people thrive from the control shame can bring. Religions are notorious for this. Most of us can think of groups who predicate righteousness by the actions of self to please divinity. It is all fine when you are performing correctly, but when you don't measure up, well . . . Rules and tenets enforced by rulers breed this culture as well, and the world Jesus entered had rule upon rule. The irony of this is the rules were meant to make men holier, but Jesus let everyone know that the worship of these rules made worship . . . worthless. While it remains true that our hearts come from a place of selfishness, once we are made new with God, Jesus is *not ashamed* to call us brothers (Hebrews 2). The irony in church circles is that we are "in sin" until we are converted to Christ, and then we are a new creation; yet many of us are inclined to feel shamed rather than *victorious* as we move forward after doing something wrong!

Culture a Catalyst

Regarding Judas's time, we must examine the clamor that was taking place among the Jews who wanted to justify themselves to the world and to Jesus. The apostles were used to bowing to the teachers of their law, so walking with a teacher who commanded respect because of a proper focus on the greater laws of love and mercy was not an easy transition. The power of the teachers of the law was their shaming of their fellow Jews. Even in the face of a man receiving sight, they scolded him that he was "steeped in sin at birth. How dare you lecture us!" (John 9). Truer shaming has never been heard, and truer cowardice has never been so exposed.

Judas grew up in a rule-focused, shame-based culture. When you are a conquered people, as the first-century Jews were, your rules and oversight of others is the only thing to hang your hat on. Judas was young, unaccomplished, and behind the curve of the other accomplished men. Am I suggesting taking all this to a point of excusing Judas? By no means! Remember, these men—great or small—all had to make real human decisions, of eternal consequence, in real time. Many would fail at the task. Judas was one who would fail, and his failure via betrayal added a layer of shame to an already frustrated frame of mind. Judas was calculating his success, staging his career, planning his mark on Judaic culture, and seeking his legacy—all in one swift action. Judas had surmised, even crystallized, his scorecard, using it as fuel for glory in what he hoped would be a self-fulfilling prophecy. It would be glorious for him and for Israel. It's just that it turned out in the polar opposite way.

When we speak careless words, we cannot take them back. When we step out on a limb and the limb breaks, we cannot retrace our steps. So it was with Judas. The deed was done. The deal he struck set eternity in motion in a way he never could have imagined. To say his actions backfired is one of the all-time understatements of the human race. By his own admission, he had betrayed innocent blood—the *only* innocent blood! He was guilty of the greater sin, and given the culture he was surrounded by, he knew he would not be able to handle the shame.

We've spoken of depression. While not necessarily conditioned on one another, depression and shame are never far apart. Once the blanket of depression has wrapped us tight, and we attempt to look into the real world to find our place, we have a half-empty glance at things, and then shame closely follows. For some, it is not a matter of stacking failure on failure, but shame itself is a constant, deadly, menacing companion.

Janice

From a very young age, Janice had contempt for life. This was because she was shamed at every turn and felt inadequate, so much so that she tried to hang herself from a swing set—at the tender age of seven. Her mother cut her down, and Janice received a beating for the act and was locked in her room for days as punishment. She grew up with beatings, a drunken mother, and unhealthy sibling relationships as a norm. This was the bedrock of her shame—acting out and, rather than finding empathy, encountering punishment.

When Janice became a Christian in her teen years, she reasoned that now she had a chance to start all over and be white as snow—but the past kept haunting her. As she put it, "Life just kept happening, and I couldn't find peace." Christianity holds such fantastic promises, but for people in a prison of shame, those promises can be hollow—or, at the very least, seem like, "They're not for me." At a person's core, there are deeply held beliefs when shame is present, and it seems that no amount of promises can touch those embedded beliefs.

> As strange as it sounds, to the soul tortured by shame, "freedom in Christ" translates to obligation, obedience, self-loathing, and self-destruction.

Janice's response to the continual pain and her personal breaking points was to hurt herself, to do the most hurtful thing she could to bring her the most shame, thereby reinforcing her internal belief system. Confessing helped reaffirm how bad she was. The pressure of a culture where people seemed to "have it all together" was too much for her. She would direct her energy to being grateful and focusing on the love of God, but she often found these things were like a foreign language. As strange as it sounds, to the soul tortured by shame, "freedom in Christ" translates to obligation, obedience, self-loathing, and self-destruction. Grace and mercy, the hallmarks of the faith, often do not apply in the mind of the shamed.

Janice continued to struggle her way through life. As she would tell me, "life" meant drugs, cancer, the love of her life developing mental illness and, finally, separation. As with many under the cloud of shame, depression, or both, life becomes useful only in what it's worth to others. So Janice lived on to care for her father and son. Once her father died, her son became sick, developing his own mental illness. He would write suicide notes; he would be placed in the hospital. Once life started its cascade, Janice made the "rational" decision that, given the trajectory she and her son were on, perhaps death was the only way to go.

A few years would pass, and her son would attempt suicide. She caught him, and not unlike her own mother, Janice would cut him down, reviving him with CPR. As if all this wasn't enough, while her son was in the hospital recovering, one night Janice was followed home by a stranger and brutally raped and mutilated. After hundreds of staples and stitches, she went home and continued moving forward—while being stalked by her assailant for months.

Later on, in his mental illness, her son tried to kill Janice. She had to let him go and has not seen him since. Evil was reinforcing her sense of shame. After all, who does all this happen to but someone *who doesn't deserve life?*

Now, with obligations gone, Janice could finally plot to end her life. This is what shame, in full bloom, does. It provides a viewpoint of life, reinforced with negative occurrences, until the person it inhabits submits to (what appears to be) the inevitable. Lethality assessments tell us that threatening self-harm, looking for various methods, thinking a plan through, talking it over, or planning it out—all of these are signs pointing to a suicide threat. Janice was at the end of this spectrum. She went to her support group one night, and learned that someone she knew there had killed himself. She saw the grieving in

the group and thought to herself, *This is what I'm going to do.*
She thought it through, and for some reason, this broke her.
Janice was beginning to change her scorecard.

On the day she had previously designated as her death day,
Janice actually ended up in the hospital, overdosed on drugs.
She decided then and there: "Literally and figuratively, I was
going to clean my room out." She threw away nearly everything in her house, isolating herself from even close friends
for two weeks. She decided to live "a deliberate life. Not one
of compulsion or obligation, but one of freedom." As she
shares now with those privileged to know her, her new apart-
ment is beautiful, housing only
herself, her dogs, and only the
objects she wants in her home.
She has wind chimes. She sits in
silence and feels the breeze. She
has stopped seeing life as her
enemy. She still hasn't escaped
the trials of this life, but not one
thought of leaving it early has
entered her mind since that key
decision and her actions that
followed.

> She decided to live "a deliberate life. Not one of compulsion or obligation, but one of freedom."

"Evil did its worst, and yet it could not break me," Janice
has said. "It could not win." For the first time in her life, "I
have tasted peace and I see God. I practice meditation and I
practice letting go. It's the first time in my life I don't resent
waking up every morning. It's the first time I'm not full of
shame or guilt and I don't need another to debase me. I have
touched evil. It has touched me. I don't know why. But I know
I'm protected."

Janice had the courage to fight when it seemed like there
was no reason to fight. She had the courage to start over, in a

most abrupt fashion and in the face of amazing odds. She has thrown out the old scorecard and replaced it with a different one. She is living a purposeful life, a simple life. Shame no longer has its grip on her.

Accepting ourselves, being comfortable in our own skin—these decisions can be extremely difficult for some. What is a no-brainer for so many can be practically impossible for others. That is what makes listening to stories like Janice's so difficult for those who are either untrained in or uneasy about such subjects. We can think that life is easy to process as long as we stick with a prescribed formula (insert: school, college, marriage, career, kids, vacations, and more).

Too often, we want to use checkers where chess-level solutions are needed. We have probably all known people—and I have advised people in this manner!—who attempted to remedy something that is much deeper than the surface with what is essentially a surface solution. It's like buffing a spot on a car where the paint and body are practically rusted away. A simple example: giving someone a canned response that "Jesus is the answer" when displayed compassion is the answer they truly need. I can't tell you how many times I've "listened" to people so that I could then talk and give a canned answer! This is totally deflating for someone who just needed a friend to listen. What's worse, in many circles, people who are unqualified to deal with something as deep as depression or shame still attempt to give pat answers rather than getting people the help they need. And the shame and depression only grow. Someone who is drowning in shame is asking for a lifeline,

> Someone who is drowning in shame is asking for a lifeline, and many times the help given to them is: "Start swimming."

and many times the help given them is: "Start swimming."

Janice's example is extreme, but extremely applicable.

It doesn't hurt to examine our life patterns every so often. Many times we surround ourselves with people who maintain unhealthy life patterns. We do what we have learned, and far too often we don't recognize the rut we are in. We can place ourselves on autopilot and default to what we know, whether those things are beneficial or not! We are suckers for familiarity. And familiarity, by the way, isn't always a bad thing—unless it's a bad thing. As strange as it may seem to someone without our specific scorecard, we may surround ourselves with those who provide the avenues, means, or encouragement to fulfill our self-destruction, or at the very least those who keep us under a glass ceiling. We interchange people, circumstances, and stimuli to prevent us from processing our life and deciding to change our scorecards to reflect where we've been, what is our healthiest path forward, and who can help us get there.

TRUE WORTH

"Mostly it is loss which teaches us about the worth of things."
—Arthur Schopenhauer[7]

For Judas, the sun had set. For the people who loved him, it would rise again. It would rise, day after day, month after month, year after year. But there would be no sound of his laughter. No sound of giggling kids as Judas chased them around the yard. No more twinkle in his eye. His mother and father would agonize. They would justify. They would seethe against their own son. They would ridicule the apostles.

And they would burn. They would burn against Jesus, burn against God, burn against any semblance of a divine plan that included the death of their son. But they would come to understand their son and what happened. Time does that. They understood his push, his drive, his youthful ignorance. Standing in the doorway, squinting at the morning sun, his mother would sigh and trudge on, day after day. Shaking the dust from the pots, swishing away the flies and gnats, keeping her home in order, and raising the remainder of her children. Life goes on.

She looked at their disheveled heads, the dirty loin cloths and coverings of busy children in the busyness of life. She would envision their big brother dutifully dusting off his siblings and sending them off with a pat on the bottom. She would have to do all this herself.

Simon would walk forward, having only a remnant of respect left in his name. It was hollow, because his son, the Jewish man's crown jewel, was gone. Gone in shame and disgrace. Judas's dreams to save Israel not only perished—along with so many other would-be saviors of that time—but his son had scarred a family for the remaining days of its generation.

Judas wasn't a martyr for the glory of Israel, like so many other messiah types. Judas was an unlikely martyr for betrayal of truth, a necessary pawn in the quest for the redemption of mankind. He was caught in a storm of his own making, a sea of dark reasoning coupled with a world thirsty for his exploitation. He died because he had to. He died because it was his destiny. He perished because the anger, fear, guilt, and shame were too much. He perished because deep down he knew Jesus' teachings would live on. And therefore we would live, too.

John

John and I spent many wonderful years together. Growing up a Midwestern boy with successful parents and a couple of younger siblings, John was always ready for fun. He would be the one jumping around, encouraging everyone to go wild. He would always be the first to go off and dance, with so many friends shaking their heads in laughter. Good old John. He hosted many a party, brought many smiles to many faces.

We met when I moved back into town. He had just graduated high school, like so many of my friends that year. We actually didn't get along much at first. Call it teenage drama, call it pride. Whatever it was, we needed to spend time away from each other even though we ran in many of the same circles. Once we'd calmed down and changed our scorecards a bit, we managed to build a great, lasting friendship. We spent many hours discussing many things, from the ends of the universe to the depths of the earth. We were college roommates, went on countless adventures, and saw amazing things. We cheated death more than once, and miraculously, we only had one encounter with law enforcement.

Once our time in college was over, we parted ways. I became a Christian and John moved back home. We remained in touch through the years. John battled many demons of addiction; at one point, he had a mild heart attack from an overdose. Yet he would sober, grow, and change into the man everyone knew he would. He grew in his career, married, and cared for his wife's kids like a champion of a man. They had a son of their own, who today is an amazing young man, talented and gifted just like his dad. Enduring accidents at work that altered him physically, John became a much-loved manager at a local bar and grill. When his back problems became too grueling, he would be stuck at home, and the demons of drug addiction he had once left behind came back.

John would struggle and ultimately give in, losing his battle with self-worth, not able to reconcile his role as someone in constant, amazing pain, and having no anchor for joy in spite of suffering. The temporary fix from medicine and other drugs would dull the pain, but only as a brief respite from the reality that remained lurking in the corner, plunging its way into everything he did. Will, a close friend of John and I, contacted us one day—Will's mother had died. We all gathered at her wake, and that was the last time most of us saw John alive. We sat together and grieved with our friend. We all shared a meal and a drink together after the funeral. It was good to spend time with John, a friend I had navigated my formative years with. We shared some laughs and taunts like the old days, but the pain was etched on John's face, and we all knew he was in a tough spot. We all lived hours apart, but maintained about as much contact as is typical of middle-aged men trying to make it in this world.

As the months wore on, John got worse. His drug problem returned in force; his confidence in himself was shot. His wife Cheryl and I talked on and off. That June, she asked me to contact him when I came to town—perhaps he would listen to me, she said. She had had enough. Later that summer I was messaging her about John's plight when she called. She had just walked in on him hanging in their bedroom. She cut him down and the race was on for the paramedics and doctors to save him. I made my way up the highway that night, and my memories began to return: this was the same route he and I took so many weekends during college to go home for visits. We shared many fun times, like the time one of us—allegedly—drove the entire two-hour trip to Lima, Ohio with his knee, terrifying the other. We had a lot of friends to visit up there, and a lot of fun every single time. Twenty years ago, neither of us would have envisioned the drive I was now making under these circumstances, a last visit to see a friend. When the exit came, I realized I was actually fine with the drive, but I didn't want to have to see what I was about to see.

After the doctor's examination, we all found ourselves sitting in a room. Cheryl, John's parents, his sixteen-year-old son, and I waited in anticipation of the doctor's verdict on John's ability to recover. To this day, it was one of the hardest moments in our lives. Then the doctor told us: it was too late. John was gone. Our shock gave way to sadness. His wife sobbed in his room. She gasped, to me and the physician on duty, "All he had to do was sit up." The doctor gave his tactless (though accurate) reply, a truth none of us understood: "He didn't want to."

We all remember John in our own way. These days, the beacons and candles are lit by random texts in the middle of the day and through memories shared on social media. Some use nature to remember and find John. Some remember his joy and believing the best in people. John loved people and music. We all shake our heads in disbelief, because he was worth so much to so many. We all can laugh at his memories, but we all know the bitterness of a life cut short. There are things we did as kids that only John and I shared, and now we cannot laugh together anymore.

We had more laughing to do. We had more stories to tell and memories to make.

His son got his driver's license. He went to prom. He went back to school. His wife found love through the pain. His siblings try to reconcile these things every day. We all do. His parents, who I have long been close with, would begin the process of sorting through the rest of their lives without their firstborn son.

Many things pass, and with each season, each memory, each of us at times mutters the same thing: "John would have loved this."

Life is deceiving to those of us who are well. That, in a given afternoon, when we are walking through the regular, even menial tasks in our lives, someone somewhere that we love very much may be processing decisions about their own existence. They may be doing this in front of and around those who can offer an ear for help, but some are doing so in the quiet of their own world.

Those who struggle with self-worth and self-doubt slosh through a twisted version of reality. Those of us who count them as having endless value

Those of us who count them as having endless value need to remember to make one more call. Send one more message. Ask one more question.

need to remember to make one more call. Send one more message. Ask one more question. True value isn't something to be quantified after it's too late, but something to be treasured in real time, with real people, in tangible ways, every day.

Make another call. Tell someone how much they mean to you. Make your day count. And help change someone's scorecard if you can.

Endnotes

1. https://www.goodreads.com/quotes/438274. The quote is found here and in many places on the Internet. Georg Christoph Lichtenberg (1742-1799) was a German scientist and satirist.

2. Barbara Kingsolver, *The Bean Trees* (New York, NY: Harper Perennial, 2013), p. 232.

3. https://www.goodreads.com/quotes/813275.

4. Roy T. Bennett, *The Light in the Heart: Inspirational Thoughts for Living Your Best Life* (Amazon Digital Services LLC, 2016), Kindle Edition.

5. Stefan Zweig, *Beware of Pity* (New York, NY: New York Review of Books, © 1976), p. 353.

6. Friedrich Nietzsche, *The Gay Science* (New York: Vintage Books, 1974), p. 220.

7. https://www.goodreads.com/quotes/250942. Arthur Schopenhauer was a German philosopher best known for his work *The World as Will and Representation*.